"I know you're mad at me," Rick said bluntly

"You haven't stopped being mad at me since you proposed to me and I turned you down—regrettably rather abruptly. I'd like to explain about that, Celia."

Her eyes sparked green fire. "I wondered how long it would take you to dredge that up." Celia spat the words. "I was a silly, infatuated schoolgirl. Nothing was further from my mind than marrying you...."

"You never were much of a liar, Celia," Rick said softly, watching her face. "It's too late to start practicing now, especially with me. I know you too well."

"You knew a schoolgirl, Rick Harland— and she certainly isn't me. I'm not a child anymore," she flung at him.

"Good," Rick said sharply. "Then perhaps we can talk like two adults about something that's important to both of us."

WELCOME
TO THE WONDERFUL WORLD
OF *Harlequin Romances*

Interesting, informative and entertaining,
each Harlequin Romance portrays an appealing
and original love story. With a varied array
of settings, we may lure you on an African safari,
to a quaint Welsh village, or an exotic Riviera
location—anywhere and everywhere that adventurous
men and women fall in love.

As publishers of Harlequin Romances, we're
extremely proud of our books. Since 1949,
Harlequin Enterprises has built its publishing
reputation on the solid base of quality and
originality. Our stories are the most popular
paperback romances sold in North America; every
month, six new titles are released and sold at
nearly every book-selling store in Canada and the
United States.

For a list of all titles currently available,
send your name and address to:

HARLEQUIN READER SERVICE,
(In the U.S.) P.O. Box 52040, Phoenix, AZ 85072-2040
(In Canada) P.O. Box 2800, Postal Station A
5170 Yonge Street, Willowdale, Ont. M2N 6J3

We sincerely hope you enjoy reading
this Harlequin Romance.

Yours truly,

THE PUBLISHERS
Harlequin Romances

A Will to Love

Edwina Shore

Harlequin Books

TORONTO • NEW YORK • LONDON
AMSTERDAM • PARIS • SYDNEY • HAMBURG
STOCKHOLM • ATHENS • TOKYO • MILAN

Original hardcover edition published in 1985
by Mills & Boon Limited

ISBN 0-373-02753-2

Harlequin Romance first edition March 1986

CHAPTER ONE

AT Heathrow her flight had been delayed for five tedious hours due to 'unfavourable circumstances for take-off'—a euphemism for the almost blizzard conditions that had swept in with the New Year and, two weeks later, showed no signs of abating. Afterwards, when with irritating cheeriness the Captain informed his wilting planeload they had been the last flight out for the day, Celia managed to dredge up a weary gratitude that she had left England at all.

There was another delay in Singapore—two hours this time and presumably par for the course since nobody had bothered with any explanations—and by the time the plane finally touched down in Sydney, Celia felt she had spent a week in transit—all of it without sleep.

Ears still buzzing, she trailed through a seemingly endless series of formalities, then in an unexpected change of tempo, was whisked along some sort of express queue past an impatient official who barely glanced into her airline carrier bag or handbag. The one hastily-packed suitcase had gone missing somewhere *en route*, and as far as Celia was concerned, could stay missing; she had lost too much valuable time already to waste more filling in batches of forms. Her only regret was that the same fate hadn't overtaken the sheepskin coat which felt like a sack of potatoes over her arm as she hurried across the Customs Hall to the nearest exit.

Celia was smiling her thanks at the young man in uniform who swung open the door for her, when the next thing she knew she was engulfed by something resembling a football crowd milling outside the doors. Noise and colour swirled around her like a *son et lumière* performance gone mad. Summer! She had forgotten. Leaving a white bitter winter in a total daze, she had not given a thought to what would be waiting for her at the other end of the flight, and now her unprepared senses reeled in protest at being flung into the blaring, dazzling brightness of an Antipodean summer.

One look at the flimsily clad suntanned bodies and Celia was instantly conscious of the weight of the thick green sweater, of the tight black cord jeans tightening ominously over her thighs . . . and the boots! Why on earth had she changed back into them just before landing? She would have been better off in the airline slippers—and looked less ridiculous at that.

With an inward groan and a deep breath she began to inch her way through the crowd, skirting a boisterous group holding up an enormous home-constructed banner which read 'Welcome Home Helen'. Lucky Helen! The thought darted involuntarily through Celia's mind. No one was waiting to meet her and since she was not expecting anyone anyway, she was annoyed by the fleeting spasm of envy. And she was not home by a long way, Celia reminded herself grimly, looking about for a sign indicating

Interstate Departures. The ladies' cloakroom
caught her eye first and after a moment's
hesitation, she made her way towards it.

Staring into the wide expanse of mirror
covering the wall of the cloakroom, Celia wished
she had spared herself the shock. The almond-
shaped eyes stared back overbright with tiredness,
the green glittering unnaturally in an ashen face
that looked completely bloodless against the
frame of dark red hair. Even the full wide mouth
was drained of colour, its upward curving corners
disappearing into the pallor of the surrounding
skin.

'I look like a ghost,' Celia wailed aloud to the
empty room as she rummaged in her handbag
and managed to find an elastic band. In a single
sweep she pulled all the hair back and caught it at
the nape in a long red tail. At least it would be
cooler than a mass of hair around her face she
told herself without much conviction, and
determinedly ignoring the reflection that looked
as if it belonged to a very tired, very vulnerable
fifteen-year-old, set off to find the Interstate
Departures.

The plane for Brisbane left on schedule. It was
the first stroke of luck to come her way and if it
held just long enough to get her to Mandarah in
time, Celia wildly promised Fate she would never
ask a favour again. An hour later, in the
reassuringly familiar Brisbane terminal she was
still bargaining with Fate under her breath as she
made her way to yet another seat allocation
counter.

For a moment Celia stood a little way back

from it, eyes skimming over the three young women on duty. In their identical pastel uniforms they looked remarkably like pretty clones and made her task unexpectedly difficult. Celia watched for a sign—any sign that would single out one of them as more approachable than the others. She flicked her eyes back to the girl with the short glossy dark curls. Was it her imagination or was that smile a shade more natural than the professional flashes of teeth of the other two?

Celia waited until the girl finished with her customer then moved forward and handed over her ticket. The girl, with a name-tag pinned to her shoulder proclaiming her as Julie, produced a fresh, genuine-looking smile. 'You've come a long way, Miss Prescott.' She picked the name off the ticket at a practised glance, bright brown eyes taking in Celia's unseasonal outfit, 'And from somewhere very cold by the look of it—you must be roasting.'

Celia raised a wry smile. 'Don't remind me.'

'The Mt Isa plane leaves in just under an hour, you won't have long to wait.' A deft flick of the wrist and one more little tag was stapled to the collection on Celia's ticket.

Celia looked directly into the girl's eyes. 'I wonder whether you could do something for me?'

'Of course.' The response was pure automation.

'I need some information—about planes from Mt Isa. You see . . .'

'Returning to Brisbane you mean?' Julie was already reaching for the schedule lying on the counter. Celia forestalled her. 'No. To Banergee Hills . . . or thereabouts.'

'Where?'

It was a familiar response. A few people had heard of the remote little outback township; the girl was not one of them and Celia wasn't surprised. 'It's south-west of Mt Isa ... it's the nearest town to where I actually want to go.'

The girl smiled, kindly. 'We don't have any commercial flights out that way—neither have the other airlines. There would only be light planes covering that area—private planes,' she explained painstakingly as if Celia had all of a sudden reverted into a dim-witted six-year-old.

You didn't grow up in outback Queensland without knowing about the mode of transport— or lack of it. With an effort Celia checked her impatience. She needed the girl's co-operation. 'I realise that. What I need to know is whether any planes—private planes, she repeated Julie's own emphasis, 'are due to fly out of Mt Isa in the general direction of Banergee Hills in the next couple of hours. I need a lift.'

Celia watched the expression on the girl's face change. Comprehension came slowly but it finally arrived. 'Oh. I see.' An apologetic smile followed. 'Well, we don't have that sort of information either—not about private planes. You'd have to check when you get to Mt Isa ... they'd have flight plans ... and things.' The professionalism faltered momentarily. 'Wouldn't they?'

'It will be another three and a half hours before I reach Mt Isa,' Celia burst out. 'And someone could be flying from there in the next hour! Don't you see? If you could telephone now for me they might wait—there might not be another plane for days ... and I need a lift now. Today. I can't afford to miss one.'

Something of her desperation had filtered through. Julie seemed genuinely regretful. 'I do understand ... really; but our airline only handles commercial traffic. They wouldn't have that information even if I did ring for you.'

She couldn't be making herself clear; that must be the problem Celia thought wearily and tried again. 'Yes, but you must know someone at the airport there whom you can ring and who'd be able to check with the right section,' she pleaded. 'I'd try myself, only ...' she shrugged, 'they probably wouldn't let me have the details. It would be better coming from you,' she persisted, knowing only too well the officialdom rampant in small country towns. She tried to gauge Julie's reaction from her frowning little face, then gave up and closed her eyes in despair.

It had been a good idea but it hadn't worked, that was all there was to it—only ... Celia wished she could be sure she wasn't going to dissolve into tears of frustration. She opened her eyes hurriedly and turned her face away while her mind raced over the alternatives. The girl was right. She would have to try and organise something when she reached Mt Isa and if she couldn't get on to a plane ...? Well, she would just have to hire a vehicle of some description and tired as she was, take on the four or five hour drive to Mandarah. It was not the end of the world, but the thought wasn't exactly cheering.

'Do you feel all right, Miss Prescott?'

Celia did not feel all right. She felt faint and for the moment, totally defeated. She met the anxious eyes. 'I'm very tired and my grandfather died,' she said disjointedly as if it explained everything then realised what she had said and could have bitten off her tongue. Sympathy from a stranger was the last thing she wanted.

Julie's face softened. 'I'm so sorry. You're on your way to the funeral . . .?'

Celia nodded vaguely, no longer caring whether the girl telephoned or not; her mind was already elsewhere.

She urgently needed to sit down—just for a moment to clear her head of the awful fuzziness, then start working on the alternatives in earnest. Would she be better off trying to hire a plane and pilot here in Brisbane, she wondered. Where would she start? She hadn't the foggiest idea. Julie was saying something. 'I beg your pardon?' Celia marshalled her concentration with an effort.

'I said I'll go into the back office and check with the manager. If he says it's okay I'll ring from there.'

The offer sank in but there was no great rush of relief. It had just hit home how fragile her reliance on picking up a lift had been. If only she had thought things through . . . contacted Mandarah to say she was coming. But she had been too shocked and in too much of a hurry for that.

'Why don't you go and sit down over there?' Julie gestured towards the waiting area nearby. 'I may be gone a while.'

The armchairs in their garish colours which

were apparently *de rigueur* for all airports, looked about as comfortable as the rack and not designed for anyone over the height of a dwarf, let alone someone who was five feet nine, with very long legs. Celia lowered herself awkwardly on to the nearest one. The noise and heat were doing terrible things to the inside of her head. What a time for the dash across the world to catch up with her, she thought miserably fighting the urge to curl up in the uncomfortable chair and go to sleep.

Ironically, the telegram had only precipitated her departure because she had already decided to come home. For the last few months she had been constantly plagued by homesickness, missing with growing desperation the harsh empty spaces of Mandarah, and her grandfather even more.

'You'll come back when you're ready,' Sam Prescott had told her and at the time Celia had been hurt that he had not stood up to George when her stepfather made his unilateral arrangements to take her away from her beloved outback. In the end, in view of what had followed, Celia couldn't leave quickly enough.

That had been four years ago. There had been visits back during the year she lived with her mother and George in Sydney. Then came the short holiday to London with her mother that had somehow turned into a stay of three years. Somehow? Who was she kidding? Celia knew exactly how it had happened. Quite simply she had been looking for an excuse not to return to Australia and had jumped at the offer of a job from Derek White, one of her Aunt Beth's

London contacts in the art world. With some misgivings, and a lot of reassurance from Derek, her mother agreed to let Celia stay on and she had felt like a puppy let off its leash.

From then on it had sort of snowballed—the receptionist job developed into a career as exhibition organiser; her circle of friends widened; she moved out of George's flat—one of his London investments, and into one of her own and life was generally great. She actually reached a stage of believing that Mandarah was emotionally behind her, as well as physically—until recently when willy-nilly, memories started nagging like a bad toothache and she found herself practically always thinking of Mandarah and the old man she hadn't seen for three years. Sam Prescott had been right: she was ready to come back—but too late. Small consolation that she might just manage to get back in time for his funeral.

'Miss Prescott.'

Celia leapt to the counter, fighting back a reluctant hope ... trying not to read too much into Julie's pleased but vaguely puzzled face.

'I'm sorry to have kept you waiting so long. It took some doing. You see——'

With an impatient shake of the head Celia cut her off. 'Is there a plane?' she demanded, unintentionally brusque.

'There's a plane flying into Mt Isa shortly. It was on its way to a place called ...' Julie dropped her eyes to the piece of paper in her hand 'Mandarah,' she said carefully, uncertain of the pronunciation 'and when they contacted the pilot on radio he said he would detour to Mt Isa to wait for you and take you on to Mandarah.' Julie looked surprised. 'He appeared to think that's where you're heading . . . it's a cattle station, isn't it?'

'Yes, yes it is,' Celia answered, breathless, and feeling even more faint from relief than from her earlier desperation. She put her handbag on the counter and drew out her purse.

'Oh no, it's all right,' Julie stammered, turning bright red in one flush. 'You needn't pay for the call or anything . . . the manager said it was okay to telephone . . . it's . . .' she broke off, helpless with embarrassment.

Celia snatched the bag off the counter, her own face flaring. She had been about to offer a tip—a sure sign that she had been away too long. She felt as embarrassed as the girl. 'Thank you. Thank you very much,' she repeated inadequately.

Julie recovered herself. 'It's probably someone flying to your grandfather's funeral, do you think . . .?'

Celia hadn't thought as far as that yet, and now that Julie mentioned it, it was a very definite possibility that the pilot, whoever he was, wouldn't be a complete stranger but some friend of her grandfather's. 'Yes, I guess it must be,' she agreed, heaping silent blessings on the unknown pilot's head with manic fervour.

Exhausted into a relieved numbness, Celia settled into the seat of yet another plane—smaller this time and with most of the oncoming passengers men. Mt Isa was a mining town and the years of travelling to and from her boarding school in Brisbane had accustomed her to travelling with a planeload of men. Celia watched them pouring into the plane, rugged, hard-muscled men with the sort of tan that wasn't picked up lying about on beaches. She caught a number of interested glances cast in her direction and suddenly realised the threat posed by the still-empty seat beside her. Hurriedly she fastened her seat belt and putting her head back, closed her eyes. She was in no mood for desultory chit-chat—or worse still, some guy doing the obligatory line.

It was too much to hope that the seat would remain empty and a minute later Celia felt someone settling into it. She recognised the motions of an experienced air traveller—no fumbling for seat-belt clasp. The movements were smooth and assured. Her eyelids flickered a little but she kept them down with a conscious effort, uneasily aware that whoever it was, was probably scrutinising her face at his leisure.

'How do you manage to look so cool in that thick sweater of yours?' The amused voice seemed right at her ear; the accent, American. Celia gave a mental sigh and opened her eyes. A slight turn of her head and she found herself looking into a pair of inquisitive light blue eyes. The smile had an easy, if practised charm about it; the face tanned beneath the cropped blond hair. His features were as regular as the numerous white teeth—capped, Celia surmised acidly.

'I hope I didn't wake you—you can't have had

time to doze off yet.' The eyes continued their summing up of her face and seemed to appreciate what they saw; the smile settled in.

Celia returned a wan smile. 'I wasn't asleep, just resting,' she said shortly, hoping he would take the hint without her needing to be too rude about it.

The smile broadened. 'Mike Johnson's the name.' He held out a hand and with no alternative but blatant rudeness, Celia gave him her own for a shake that turned out to be too long by half.

'My name is Celia,' she said, grudgingly, tugging her hand out of his clasp and prickling with annoyance at being inveigled into acquaint-anceship against her will. 'I'm afraid I'm very tired, so if you'll excuse me.' She put her head back without giving him a chance to comment and shut her eyes in discouragement, which was as far as she could go without actually spelling out that that was where the acquaintanceship ended.

She had not meant to fall asleep. When she opened her eyes again Celia felt disorientated and needed a few moments to remember which particular plane she was on this time. Something about the settled atmosphere inside the plane told her she had been asleep for some time. She stole a tentative glance at Mike and discovered he was watching her obliquely through his sandy lashes.

Completely unabashed at having been caught staring, he grinned. 'Good nap? Boy, you went out like a light. You really must have been done in. How far have . . .?'

'Just from England.' Celia anticipated the question abruptly, and sprung her own before he had a chance to react. 'And what about you? Are you connected with the mines at Mt Isa?' She smiled invitingly, to distract him.

His curiosity about her diverted—for the moment at least—Mike rose to the bait. 'In a manner of speaking, yes. What I mean is I'm in the mining industry, but not exactly connected with the organisation that runs Mt Isa Mines— we're a different outfit. I'll be staying in Mt Isa a while though—worse luck,' he tossed in with a rueful grin.

She knew that was meant to be her cue to ask why he found the idea so unattractive but didn't care enough to confirm her own inmpression that he was strictly a big-city man. Mike confirmed it for her anyway.

'Not exactly a jumping place, is it?' He gave a sour laugh.

Celia shrugged non-committally and his expression underwent instant change to project mock horror, absurdly overdone. 'Say, don't tell me you live there—I didn't mean to imply that it's not okay—what I meant was . . .'

'I don't live there.' Celia cut into what threatened to be a long and boring extrication from his supposed *faux pas*. 'I'm going on from there to stay . . . on a property,' she volunteered, reluctantly.

'Better you than me. I'll be dropping by one of those ranches—stations or whatever you call them here. Not by choice mind you—business. I'm a negotiator.' He added the last bit with naïve pride and Celia could have sworn he puffed out his chest as he said it.

Having no idea what the term meant she was hardly impressed. 'Really?' she said with a vague frostiness. Something about his manner was starting to remind her dreadfully of her step-father.

Only a very wide cultural gap could have made him read interest into her mechanical response. 'Yeah, really,' Mike launched off earnestly. 'A property will be coming up on the market any day now and my company is getting first option on it. There's a range of hills on the edge of the place that are worth looking into . . .' He paused to chuckle at his corny pun and Celia felt obliged to jerk her mouth at the corners to indicate that she'd caught on. 'I'm here to start off the negotiations in the next couple of days,' Mike went on. 'Get the ball rolling—talk money and all that . . . then the heavies take over—solicitors, accountants . . . but it's me who gets it all going— the negotiations,' Mike explained enthusiastically.

'I see.' Balls rolling . . . talk money. It was George in disguise. Celia felt a laugh rising in her throat and coughed to strangle it in its tracks.

Mike was watching her closely. 'Say, I was wondering . . . when we touch down, if you're not in a hurry we might . . .'

It had to come sooner or later. 'I'm being met.' Celia stepped in briskly, stretching the truth a little, 'And flying straight on . . . to the property.' Instinctively she avoided mentioning Mandarah by name. While she did not really expect him to come ferreting her out, her sense of privacy recoiled from supplying even such meagre

information about herself to a perfect stranger—
and one she was quite certain she would dislike
on further acquaintance.

'Too bad.' Mike's face fell—momentarily. 'But
what about when you get back to Brisbane?'
Evidently he was not the type to be put off
easily—a handy trait in a negotiator. Celia gave a
tepid smile. 'I'm afraid I don't know when I'll be
coming back,' she said firmly and would have
said it anyway to block off further overtures, but
it did happen to be the truth.

She had not thought any further than the
funeral and all her mental energy had been
concentrated into getting herself to Mandarah in
time for that. Afterwards? She had vague
thoughts of staying on at Mandarah for a while if
grandfather's sister Addie had no objections.
Otherwise when she tried to think about the
future, there was a very large, very determined
block in her mind.

'Is there anywhere I can contact you?' Mike
had been studying her averted face. Celia turned
to him. 'I'd like to, Celia.' His eyes lingered into
hers for an annoyingly long moment.

'No.' Celia stared back without blinking.

Mike reached into the inside pocket of his
jacket. 'Well, I'll give you my card anyway, and if
you find yourself in Brisbane in the next couple
of weeks, I'll expect you to call me. Oh, and
there's a Sydney number on it too—you can get
in touch with me there if you're down that way.'

And pigs might fly. She could hear George in
his every word. Celia took the card and slipped it
into her handbag without glancing at it.

Mike looked past her through the window. 'Looks like we're landing.'

'Not before time,' Celia muttered under her breath. Mike's casual assumption that she'd be falling over herself to get in touch with him had her bristling with indignation.

The canned music came on as they taxied to a stop. A hostess, all teeth and charm as canned as the music, retrieved Celia's coat from the overhead rack and held it out with a faintly amused lift of an eyebrow. 'Yours, I think?' she said sweetly, flicking her eyes over Celia's unconventional outfit.

Mike leapt to his feet and took the coat before Celia had a chance to reach out a hand. 'I'll carry it for you,' he volunteered with cheerful gallantry.

Resisting the temptation to tell him he could keep it, Celia followed him down the aisle.

A wall of incredibly hot, humid air hit her in the face as she stepped through the doorway of the plane. It was like walking slap-bang into a sauna fully clothed and the unexpectedness of it made Celia give a gasp of shock. The usual covered walkway into the terminal building was not a feature of country airports; the wheeled-up steps led straight down on to the tarmac, and in this case, a tarmac that radiated a steamy heat after an obviously recent downpour.

Celia braced herself. Mike was already waiting for her at the bottom of the steps, clutching her enormous coat in one hand, his briefcase in the other, both looking slightly ludicrous as accessories to his rather curious version of a short-sleeved navy safari suit. Not half as curious as her own gear—and a lot cooler. Celia wished herself half so lucky.

He grimaced when she reached him. 'Warm, wouldn't you say?' he said with sarcastic understatement. 'And you wonder why I can't stand the place.'

She hadn't wondered any such thing but mustered a feeble smile of commiseration, saving her breath for the trek. The familiar outline of the terminal beckoned like an oasis in a desert across the black stretch of bitumen. Beads of perspiration were already breaking out on her forehead and Celia could feel a clammy dampness at the back of her neck where the tail of hair pressed down on the sweater. Halfway across, an ominous wavy sensation started swirling around in her head. Celia kept her eyes rigidly fixed on the low-lying building ahead.

'You okay?' Mike queried sharply. 'You look kinda pale—paler, that is,' he amended, clearly meaning white as a sheet.

Celia nodded and got a fright as the ground tilted erratically from the too sudden movement of her head.

'You want to get yourself out of that gear as quickly as you can—it's not really the thing for this sort of weather,' Mike advised solemnly.

He had to be joking! Celia glanced at him to see whether he was serious. Mike looked back, face showing nothing but a stolid concern. He wasn't joking. She checked a half-hearted giggle. Did he actually think she normally travelled rigged up like an Eskimo in blazing heat just for the fun of it—or as a conversation opener? Of course she intended changing out of her woollen strait-jacket at the first opportunity. She was relying on finding some leftovers hanging in her old wardrobe that might be resurrected into service. It was unlikely that Addie, a hoarder all her life, would have brought herself to throw anything out.

Within a few yards of the glass doors into the terminal, Celia faltered in her stride, eyes riveted in disbelief on a figure on the other side of the tinted glass, then recovering herself, gave a strangled laugh at the trick her mind had played on her. Hallucinating, that's what she was doing! Heat and utter exhaustion had momentarily catapulted her frazzled brain back to the times she was coming home from boarding school for the holidays and Rick Harland was waiting to fly her to Mandarah.

'What's up? You look as if you've just seen a ghost.' Mike swung open the door and the figure, no longer behind glass, zoomed into focus. Rick Harland, very definitely not a ghost, moved towards them. Celia felt the blood sweep from her face and an odd rickety sensation around the knees. Later, she wondered if her mouth had actually dropped open like a stunned child's.

In a way, everything about Rick was as she remembered, only stronger, more definite, as if the picture she had been carrying in her mind during the last four years had been a fuzzy photograph. In real life Rick was taller, more powerfully built. The angular features were more sharply defined—possibly because the curling

hair was closer cropped than the last time she'd
seen him. It looked darker too—almost as black
as the T-shirt he had tucked into the jeans.

She had got the grey eyes exactly right though.
They travelled unnervingly slowly over her white
face as she continued to stare, still wide-eyed
with disbelief. Then Rick's mouth curved slightly
in a familiar lopsided tilt. 'Hello, Celia,' he said
softly, and the deep drawling voice had the effect
of physically brushing her skin. Celia flinched.

In her mind she had rehearsed this meeting
hundreds of times—she, very cool, terribly
sophisticated; her first comment devastatingly
cutting. 'Hello, Rick.' Her voice was ghastly—a
squeaking-over-glass sort of sound. She was
seventeen again and any poise or sophistication
she might have acquired since their last meeting
vanished without a trace.

'We're blocking the doorway.' Mike brought
the tableau to life. Celia turned to him, quite
astonished to find he was still there. The sight of
Rick had wiped Mike completely from her mind.

They moved away from the doorway, a few
steps into the arrival lounge, then just stood
there as if no one knew what to do next. Mike's
eyes moved rapidly from her to Rick then settled
back on her. Celia frowned. Was he waiting
for her to introduce them . . .? 'Rick Harland,
Mike Johnson,' she murmured, and watched as
they gave each other curt nods of acknowledge-
ment, neither extending a hand, although they
seemed to stare a little harder at each other.
Celia recognised a sizing-up look when she saw
one.

Mike was about her own height so Rick had the advantage of at least four inches which he used effectively. Mike drew himself up almost to attention under the cold stony-grey appraisal that would have frosted glass. 'Well, I guess I'll be on my way,' he said with a painful attack of cheeriness, jumping feet first to the conclusion that Rick had been waiting to meet her. And that suited Celia just fine—for the moment.

With an abrupt gesture Mike pushed her coat at Rick who took it mechanically in the way people do when something is shoved into their hands unexpectedly, but Celia noted the flicker of surprise in his eyes, and realised Rick had jumped to his own conclusion—that Mike was travelling with her.

'Thanks, Mike,' she said, and wondered what it was she was thanking him for—for carrying her coat, she supposed, since there was nothing else.

'I'll be expecting to hear from you, Celia,' he smiled, brightly, and for too long, then flashed Rick a look that bordered on the defiant. In that moment the naïve conceit, mildly irritating on the plane, made Celia seize up with fury.

As she watched Mike's slim shoulders disappearing into the huddle around the luggage trolleys, she had a mad urge to explain him away to Rick—to say that she'd only met Mike on the plane and hoped never to see him again. She turned to Rick, the words on the tip of her tongue—and caught herself just in time. She owed Rick Harland no explanations about Mike or anything else.

Rick looked up from frowning at the bundle of

suede and fur in his arms. Just one reference
to her gear and she would scream—really scream.
Celia beamed the threat in a glare as their
eyes met. Rick gave a low whistle under his
breath. 'My God, you've come straight from
London!'

'Congratulations!' Celia shot back tartly. 'Your
powers of deduction are mind-boggling—although it wasn't quite as straight as a Mandarah
crow flies.'

There she was at last—as cutting as in the best
of her fantasy rehearsals, but as her grandfather's
favourite old phrase slipped out, a vivid image of
the wiry, sunburnt old man flickered in front of
her eyes, and everything went very still. She
looked desperately into Rick's watching eyes. 'I
should have been there.' The words wrenched
themselves out in a jagged whisper. Celia blinked
hard and averted her face quickly.

The next moment she was held to a hard,
broad chest, Rick's arm tightly around her
shoulder. She took a deep sighing breath and
slackened wearily against him, her mind blissfully
blank for about half a minute before awareness
pushed through the numbness. What was she
doing in Rick Harland's arms? Celia jerked out of
them angrily and stepped back so quickly she
would have tripped if Rick hadn't gripped her
arm to steady her. He dropped his hand almost
instantly. 'I'm fine now. Thank you,' Celia
muttered, confused and shaken to have needed
that short moment of comfort in his arms.

'I'm sorry about Sam,' Rick said, a certain
stiffness in his voice making his words sound

impersonally formal.

Celia gave a brief nod and looked around distractedly. 'There's someone waiting for me—to fly me to Mandarah. The girl at the airline desk said he'd wait,' she started to explain, clutching at the genuine excuse to get away from Rick before she said or did anything else that would expose her vulnerability.

'I'm the one waiting for you,' Rick said quietly and although she heard him clearly enough, her eyes continued their search of the lounge. Her mind was not exactly working at top speed but the message did get through eventually. She swung back to Rick. 'Yes, but . . .' she stopped. 'You're the pilot . . .?' Rick inclined his head a fraction. 'But the girl didn't say—she should have told me,' Celia blurted idiotically.

Rick gave a curious smile. 'Next time you'll know to ask,' he said softly, then in a change of voice said, 'Come on, I'll get your case and grab some sandwiches for you to eat on the plane. I'd like to take off pretty much immediately.'

'My case has gone missing and I'm not hungry so I needn't hold you up,' Celia snapped with unnecessary tartness to hide her agitation at this unexpected turn of events.

Rick had her arm and was already guiding her towards the cafeteria. 'I don't want any sandwiches!' she protested and was appalled at how peevishly childish she sounded. What was the matter with her? Why was it she seemed hell-bent on making Rick believe she was still the hopelessly unsophisticated adolescent of their last encounter . . .? 'I won't eat them!' Her voice rose alarmingly, the last of her self-possession hanging by a thread.

'Then you can feed them to the crows at Mandarah,' Rick said calmly. 'So shut up.'

CHAPTER TWO

In the end Celia ate the indifferent sandwiches with an embarrassingly obvious appetite that sprang up from nowhere. When she had finished, she put her head back and did her best to feign sleep. It wasn't easy; the humidity in the compact cabin made her skin prickle and itch so badly under the heavy sweater it was all she could do to stop herself wrenching the wretched garment off her back. Another minute and she would have to sit up to get some relief.

How long had they been in the air? She didn't want to blow her cover by a surreptitious peek at her watch but her senses told her it couldn't possibly be more than half an hour, which meant the best part of another hour and a half to endure.

It would be a long time before she bargained with Fate again; she might have guessed there'd be a price exacted for the lift she needed so desperately, but who'd have predicted it would turn out to be two hours trapped in the air with Rick Harland of all people? Celia was still much too angry at her own idiotic behaviour to appreciate the neatness of the irony. Shock or no shock, she should have kept a better grip on herself and not lurched into Rick's arms like some miserable kid—and then to have topped that off with near enough to a fit of the tantrums because she didn't want to eat! She couldn't have made a bigger fool of herself if she'd tried.

Celia tossed up whether to break the silence with a reference to her state of shock—something to get across that she had acted out of character, but decided against it. Her nerves were not up to the job; every time she opened her mouth something stupid came out. They had not exchanged a word since Rick handed her the plastic-wrapped packet of sandwiches and she had forced out a frosty 'thank you', and the best thing she could do was hold her tongue.

Her back was tormenting her. Celia tried to shift position as inconspicuously as she could. How long now?

'Why don't you take that stupid thing off?' Rick's tart voice interrupted her mental calculation of passing seconds. Celia bit back a retort.

Rick wasn't fooled for a moment. 'Why bother pretending? I know you're not asleep. You're being driven out of your mind by that bear rug on your back. Do yourself a favour and take it off.'

'Don't be ridiculous!' She rose to the bait and snapped back without looking at him, but sat up anyway. Out of the corner of her eye she caught the abrupt movement of Rick's head towards her and stared stonily ahead.

'If you reach behind you to the back seat and lay your hands on my overnight bag, you'll find a clean T-shirt in there that you can put on. I wasn't suggesting you sit here entirely topless,' Rick said wryly. 'Not unless you prefer to, of course,' he added with mock courtesy.

Celia caught back an exclamation. The fierce rush of hostility brought a hot pulsating spot to each cheek. After a long pause she said, icily, 'I'm quite comfortable as I am.'

She should have expected he wouldn't be able to resist raking that up, but was taken aback because she simply wasn't prepared for it. And even if the dig had not been intentional it found its mark anyway, and the humiliatingly graphic picture reared in her mind. Celia saw herself as she had been the last time they were together—well and truly topless, and felt the old nausea churning away in her stomach at the memory of what had followed.

'Celia?'

Celia kept her face rigidly away from him, staring blankly into the blueness outside the passenger window, waiting for the sick feeling to pass and for the malicious memories to slip back into whatever storage box they lived in in her mind—until the next time some passing comment let them loose again.

Rick made a sound of impatience. 'I didn't mean anything by my comment,' he said stiffly, 'so don't go reading things into it that weren't there.'

So he knew his remark had struck home. How transparent she must be! 'I don't know what you're talking about,' Celia lied grimly through clenched teeth, cursing her own vulnerability.

'Have you stayed angry with me all these years?' Rick asked, so softly that Celia almost missed hearing the question.

Angry? Yes, she had stayed angry all right—

and hurt, but she had no intention of telling him that. If Rick thought she was ready to start blithely discussing how awful she had felt—still felt about what happened by the river four years ago, he had better think again.

'I tried to see you in Sydney—several times,' Rick said pointedly, 'but you must know that.'

She did know that because he had made the mistake of telephoning to say he was coming. Luckily she had never been the one who had answered the 'phone. The message had always been passed on though, and Celia had always made damned sure she was miles away from the house whenever Rick was due.

'You were always very busy—somewhere else,' Rick sounded curiously offended. If she didn't know better, she might have said, hurt.

'And why shouldn't I have been? I was leading a very busy life,' Celia snapped crossly, goaded into answering by the unaccountable tone of Rick's voice, when her instincts warned her not to be drawn into discussion. There was too much thin ice over the past.

'Doing what?' Rick countered.

Celia hesitated, then went ahead with her fib. 'Having fun,' she said airily and ignored the quizzical jerk of Rick's dark brows. So what if he didn't believe her? And it was not a complete lie. There had been some good times ... parties and discos and long, lazy days on beaches—but not enough to counteract the bouts of excruciating boredom in between, nor the gnawing sense of uselessness and frustration that made her want to scream. Basically, she'd had a lousy time at

George's until she had started working in Aunt Beth's art gallery. Even then, she wasn't deliriously happy, but at least she had been busy and had genuinely liked her job as her aunt's girl-Friday. 'I was working too, of course,' she announced, smugly.

'Of course,' Rick repeated drily. 'Sam told me.'

The comment was so casually tossed in that it took a few moments for its implication to sink in, and then it made Celia catch her breath. And what else had her grandfather told Rick? An uncomfortable warmth spread into her cheeks at the thought that any part of her letters, even edited versions, might have filtered through to Rick. Did he know how utterly miserable she had been after leaving Mandarah? Celia shifted uneasily in her seat.

'You'd be more comfortable without that sweater,' Rick suggested again and Celia was so thankful he put her fidgeting down to mere physical discomfort that she was only too anxious to confirm it. 'I am a bit hot, but I'll be all right, thanks. We should be there soon anyway,' she said, quite brightly.

'Please yourself.' Rick didn't press the point. He glanced at her briefly. 'They're going to be very surprised to see you—I don't think anyone is expecting you to turn up out of the blue like this.'

'Not expecting me? Of course Addie's expecting me! She sent me the telegram.'

'I didn't mean Addie—I meant the others.'

'Who? Mother and George?'

'For a start, Eleanor and George, yes.' The

nuance of distaste in Rick's voice was unmistakable.

Years ago, with nothing more than instinct to go by, Celia had concluded that Rick did not like her mother and after her father's death from a fall off his horse eight years ago, it seemed to Celia that Rick went deliberately out of his way to avoid Eleanor. When, after only five months of widowhood her mother married George Carr and moved to Sydney, Rick scarcely mentioned her and never asked after her. His attitude towards George could be summed up as stonily civil, but he loved Addie—most people did, provided they were allowed past the caustic exterior that was just a front for a genuinely kindly nature.

'Addie must be taking it hard,' Celia murmured, her heart going out to the old lady in her loss.

'No,' Rick said firmly. 'At least not Sam's death—she had long enough to get ready for that and he went peacefully. The contingent of official mourners is a bit hard to take though,' he added grimly.

'Were you there when . . .?'

Rick turned his head to her questioning eyes. 'When Sam died?' He finished off what she couldn't bring herself to say. 'Yes, I was there,' he said, with no emotion whatsoever, and a stranger might have thought the curiously detached voice indicated a callous indifference. Celia knew that was not true; Rick had loved Sam.

She looked away, and glancing down, saw Rick's knuckles were quite white on the controls.

Strangely, the sight only increased the animosity she felt towards him. Rick had no right to edge into that part of her life. Sam had been her grandfather—the person she had loved most in the world after her father and she should have been with him at the end, not Rick. Without warning, her bottom lip began to tremble badly, and for an unnerving moment Celia thought she was going to cry. She bit into the lip savagely, conscious that Rick was watching her. She sensed his sympathy—or was it empathy? Whatever it was she couldn't stand it, nor the heavy silence that had distended into minutes. Grasping the first thought that came into her head she voiced it with a grotesque display of brightness. 'What a coincidence—you flying by! What were you doing in Brisbane?'

'I was in Sydney actually—raising money.' Rick answered so curtly that Celia felt she had been caught snooping into his personal affairs.

'I wasn't prying,' she said in a flush of self-defence, then risked asking, 'Was it a bad year?' Grandfather's letters had made no mention of any prolonged drought during the last couple of years—of dry spells yes, but not the kind that sent property owners cap in hand to bank managers.

'If you're talking about the weather, we haven't had any drought—in fact there's been much too much rain about and some of the rivers are already in flood and too close for comfort. Dad's place is safe enough for the moment, thank God—so is Mandarah.'

If it wasn't the elements turning against the

Harlands Celia couldn't guess what it was, and was not about to risk a snub by asking. She hoped, quite sincerely, they weren't in financial difficulties because with one obvious exception, she was very fond of them, although it was literally years since she had seen either Rick's parents or his younger brother, John.

'The reason I've been raising money is to be able to buy Mandarah,' Rick said slowly and very distinctly, as if speaking to someone of limited intelligence—and hard of hearing at that.

Celia had just been about to ask after his family thinking it a safe enough subject to broach. Rick's statement pushed everything out of her mind in one swish. 'What?'

'You heard.'

Oh, she had heard all right, only couldn't believe she had heard correctly. Celia found her voice at last. 'You've got to be joking!' Celia gave a little laugh from sheer shock. 'Addie would never sell—never! You know her as well as I do. She'd never give up Mandarah—not for all the money in the world—not even to you. It's her life . . . it's . . .' Celia ran out of steam. Incredulous, she scrutinised Rick's impassive profile, searching for some clue to his crazy statement in the hard set of the mouth and jaw. They told her nothing.

Rick turned to her, his face unreadable. 'Hasn't it occurred to you that it may not be up to Addie to decide what happens to Mandarah?' he asked, painstakingly, allowing each word time to sink in.

Celia stared at him blankly.

Rick's lips twisted into a grim smile. 'Obviously

not, I see. Well, I'd start thinking about it now, if I were you.'

Her brows were knitting together with the effort of trying to make sense of what Rick was saying. Was she so travel-weary and stupid that she didn't have the remotest inkling of what he was talking about? She couldn't take her eyes off his face in case she missed some hidden clue. 'Think about it, Celia,' Rick suggested, casually, turning back to his controls.

'Think about what? I don't understand what you're on about, Rick,' she cried out plaintively and could have hit him when he didn't answer.

Celia gave an angry shrug and swung her own face to the window. What was she supposed to think about?—that Mandarah could possibly be put up for sale . . .? The idea was so preposterous that Rick was either out of his mind, or playing some sort of mean game with her for his own devious ends. It wouldn't be the first time he had played on her naïvety. Celia pressed her forehead against the window. The glass felt like ice against the heat of her forehead.

Below them, etched against the darkening horizon, lay the familiar range of hills that bordered the Mandarah property on one side. Celia let out a small, audible sigh of relief. They were home. No, she was the one who was home, she amended the thought smartly and if Rick Harland had ideas of making it his home, he would find himself with a fight on his hands.

'We're home,' Rick said lightly as he brought the plane down on to the small landing strip a short way from the collection of sprawling buildings that made up the homestead. Celia froze. Did he say that on purpose? Probably not, but nevertheless she was peeved. 'Yes, I am,' she enunciated frigidly, overdoing the emphasis so madly that Rick tossed her a startled glance.

'Thank you for the lift.' Politeness dragged out the stiff phrase grudgingly. Without waiting for Rick to come around to open the door for her Celia scrambled out of the plane and then had to wait, seething with impatience while Rick took his time getting her few bits and pieces from the back seat. 'I'll take them.' She reached for the airline bag and coat, fretting to be rid of him, then saw that as well as her things, Rick had his own overnighter tucked under his arm. 'Why are you bringing that? Are you staying the night?'

'I've been staying here off and on for a month or so now,' Rick said off-handedly.

Her first reaction was another charge of resentment that he should have been making himself so much at home—in her home. The nasty jolt came a moment later. 'You were here helping Grandfather before he died!' Accusing Rick of murdering the old man could not have sounded worse. Celia was appalled at her own rudeness.

'Someone had to,' Rick said, tight-lipped, and pushing past her without apology, started striding towards the main house. The set of his back told her he was furious.

Celia caught up and fell into step beside him. She wanted to apologise, only nothing sounded right in her head—maybe because of all the confused resentment still swirling around in there. 'You've been very kind and I ...' she ventured lamely in a tight, prim voice. Illogically furious with Rick for making it so hard for her, she shrugged, muttering, 'You know what I mean.'

'I didn't do it for you, Celia, so you don't have to twist yourself into knots forcing yourself to feel grateful,' Rick retaliated savagely, then suddenly stopped dead in his tracks. Automatically Celia stopped too, without knowing what they were stopping for.

'Hell, Celia, I'm sorry. I didn't mean to bite your head off.' Rick's voice was saturated with weariness.

She looked him full in the face then, and it was as if she was seeing him for the first time—really seeing the lines of tension marking out the bones in his face, the unaccustomed shadows under the grey eyes—and it shocked her. Rick was every bit as exhausted as she was. The realisation set off a wave of involuntary compassion. She managed a quick half smile that was no more than an upward jerk of the lips. 'It's okay, we're both tired.'

Rick gave a fleeting nod. 'Take it easy tomorrow, Celia, don't let them get to you,' he said gently, and while it may have been a trick of the fading light, Celia thought she saw something like concern in his eyes. She found it unaccountably disturbing and dropped her eyes quickly.

Although it was barely nine o'clock, only George appeared to be still up, materialising drink in hand through the double doors of the living room as they stepped into the wide hall. Like a squat, overweight buddha in his short scarlet silk robe, he looked even less prepossessing than Celia remembered, but then, she was usually spared the sight of his short stumpy legs.

The last time she had seen her stepfather was about six months ago when he and her mother had passed through London. They were always passing through somewhere—staying just long enough for George to check on his numerous investments, and for her mother to take in the shops at the breathless pace she seemed to thrive on.

'Good grief! What are you doing here?'

Charm was not one of her stepfather's strong points. Celia was much too tired to react. 'I'm here for the funeral,' she answered wearily.

An ugly stream of dark red rose up along George's thick neck and meandered unevenly into the jowly cheeks. 'Yes, yes of course,' George nodded rapidly, making the light flick off the top of his bald head. 'Sorry about the old man and all that,' he muttered, the closest to abashed Celia could remember. 'Just didn't expect to see you, that's all. Eleanor didn't tell me you were coming.'

'Mother didn't know.' Celia turned to Rick. 'Thank you, I'll take those now . . .'

'I'll take them to your room.' Rick tossed George a sharp look catching him staring with unconcealed curiosity and fairly open dislike. 'I suppose Celia's room is still free?' He arched an interrogatory eyebrow.

'Of course it's free. We didn't exactly turn up in hordes,' George bridled.

'Good,' Rick returned shortly. 'Try and sleep

in tomorrow,' he told Celia. 'The service doesn't
start until ten so we don't need to take off until
well after nine. The others will be driving off
earlier,' he added pointedly, without giving
George a second glance.

'Arrogant b . . .' George muttered under his
breath as he glared at Rick's back receding down
the long, central corridor. 'He knows I couldn't
get hold of a plane to take us all into Banergee
Hills for the funeral—it wouldn't hurt him to
offer to do a couple of trips in his plane.' He
swung his attention abruptly back to Celia. 'You
want a drink? You look bushed.' He eyed her up
and down. 'And what in blazes are you doing in
that crazy gear?'

Resisting the charmless hospitality without
effort and ignoring the rest, Celia said coldly,
'I'm very tired and would rather go straight to
bed, thank you.'

The airy, spacious room was as Celia had last
left it. She stood in the doorway taking in the
reassuringly dear cream and blue-toned scene and
felt she had opened a magic door into a warm
secure childhood—and yet it hurt; the sharp
painful jab somewhere below her ribs told her
there was no door back into the past and she was
a fool for succumbing to the illusion—even if
only for the briefest of moments.

As she entered the room, her eyes fell on the
small vase of flowers on the bedside table. A
lump rose to her throat. Darling Addie was
expecting her even if no one else was. And who
else had turned up? She had not followed up
Rick's sarcastic comment about a contingent of

official mourners, and now that, together with his pointed question to George about her room, aroused a lukewarm curiosity. She was too tired to pursue it and decided she could wait until the next morning to find out. Apart from Addie, there was no one she particularly wanted to see.

Rick had left her bag and coat on the bed and disappeared—she assumed to the self-contained manager's wing, because that seemed the most likely place for him to have installed himself for a prolonged stay. Relieved that there was no risk of coming across him in the main house, Celia dropped her handbag on to the bed beside the other things, peeled off the boots that had practically glued themselves to her feet, and headed out of the room again, to the bathroom at the end of the short passage.

She would have loved a long wallow in luxuriantly hot, scented water to soak off the layers of grime and perspiration, not to mention the tension, that had seeped into every pore of her body. Celia eyed the deep tub longingly, and actually got as far as turning on the tap before it occurred to her that what she really craved was simply falling into bed; and the shortest route to that was via the shower cubicle.

She had her shower, then with a large towel secured around her, doing service as a robe, and the clothes under her arm, she padded back to her room.

Adele Prescott rose slowly from the bed, pulling the shabby cotton robe around her thinness.

Just for a moment Celia hesitated in the

doorway, then with a muffled cry she dropped everything to the floor and flung herself into the old lady's arms.

Addie's dry, bony hand raked awkwardly over Celia's wet hair, while the other clasped her fiercely around the bare shoulder, and for the first time since receiving that telegram Celia let the tears flow unchecked in a steady, silent stream down her cheeks. The relief was physical; it felt as if all the knotted up tension was flowing out with the tears.

'There there, it's all right, Celia child, it's all right.'

Celia pulled away with a jerk. 'It's not all right Addie—not anymore. Nothing will ever be all right again,' she contradicted in a mixture of anger and despair. 'You don't understand—it's all changed,' Celia railed like a child, the tears streaming down her cheeks.

Addie fished out a handkerchief from the pocket of her robe and pushed it into Celia's hand. 'Come on, that's enough. Blow your nose now.'

Celia dabbed viciously at the tears and blew her nose as ordered.

Addie picked up a faded cotton nightgown off the bed. 'Here, put this on, you'll catch a chill in that wet towel. Rick told me you lost your case so I've looked out a few things for you—I'll dig out some more tomorrow.'

Celia let herself be bundled into the nightdress and a navy towelling robe which had seen better days. 'That's more like it,' Addie said approvingly, and taking Celia's hand, led her to the bed. She sat down beside her. 'Don't be so miserable child.'

'I should have come before, Addie ... I ...' Celia started.

'You've come now, that's enough,' Addie cut her off.

'But I meant to come home earlier—I was going to come back, really I was,' Celia persisted. 'I didn't mean to stay away so long.' It seemed terribly important to explain to the old lady why she had stayed away so long. If Addie could forgive her she might be able to start forgiving herself.

'I said that's enough Celia,' Addie stopped her sternly, her high, dry voice crackling. 'I know you cared about Sam and he knew it too. You didn't have to be here to love each other. You had your reasons for staying away, and remember Sam wanted you to go away in the first place. He knew you'd come back when it was time. He was a wise man and it would be a wilfully cruel thing if you let guilt mar your memories of him—and the good times.' She gave Celia's hand a squeeze. 'You're too sensible for that.'

'Am I?' Celia asked doubtfully. Sensible? She had never envisaged herself as that. Stubborn, George always called her when he wasn't calling her hot-headed.

'Yes, certainly you are.' A flicker of a smile crossed Addie's weather-beaten face. 'You always did have a good dose of the Prescott common sense—which is more than I can say for some.' The belligerence was so familiar that Celia smiled in spite of herself. 'And your sister is not

improving with age, the scatter-brain! Still as
frivolous and vain as ever—only worse, if that's
possible.'

A thought struck home. 'You can't be telling
me that Lucy is here too?' Celia asked slowly.

Addie nodded, smiling a grim little smile. 'Oh,
yes, they're all here—with bells on.'

'But why?' It didn't make much sense to Celia.
Her sister had fled Mandarah when she turned
sixteen to stay with Aunt Beth in Sydney before
making her way in the world of modelling. When
she left, Lucy had sworn all the wild horses in
Queensland couldn't bring her back, and Celia
could count Lucy's fleeting visits in the interven-
ing years on the fingers of one hand. Lucy hated
the Outback as much as their mother did, if not
more, and as for her feelings towards Sam ...
Lucy simply didn't have many feelings to spare
for anyone after she had lavished the bulk of
them on herself.

Frowning, she met Addie's grey eyes. Age
had made them peculiarly opaque, giving them
a soft, chalky look, but the glint of shrewd
amusement was unmistakable. Addie gave a wry
twist of her thin lips. 'The will child, the will.'
And as Celia's brows rose in astonishment, the
old lady chuckled. 'Nothing like the death of a
very rich man to bring so-called family scurry-
ing in from the far-flung corners of the
globe—don't be daft child,' she snapped as
Celia dropped her eyes, 'I didn't mean you and
you know it. Oh yes, they're all here—that
uppity Beth and her namby-pamby husband ...
interior decorator he calls himself. How a

grown man can play around with cushions and
bits of fluff and say it's a job is beyond me.'

'The Laceys—Beth and Julian. Here ...
Now ...?'

'Yes, they're here too.' Addie touched Celia's
cheek with a work-roughened hand. 'Don't let
them get to you, Celia girl, particularly that loud-
mouthed George.' She repeated Rick's earlier
advice almost word for word. 'It will be a long
hard day tomorrow, so you'd best get a good
night's sleep. Rick will fly us over to Banergee
Hills—the others can draw lots for the fourth
seat,' she cackled drily, then looked serious—and
sad. 'Bless him, I don't know what I would have
done without Rick. You're glad to see him again,
aren't you?' Addie asked suddenly, catching Celia
off-guard. Celia opened her mouth and shut it
again. Addie answered her own question. 'Of
course you are—you were always so fond of him,
and I know Rick has missed you. You can't have
seen each other since ...' She drew all the
wrinkles on her forehead down into a multi-
layered frown of concentration. 'Let me see ...
Rick said he didn't get to see you in London, so it
must have been as long ago as that Christmas.'
She smiled indulgently into Celia's tightly
controlled face as the younger woman almost
started at the mention of Rick in London. When
had he been there? And why hadn't he mentioned it? Why should he have mentioned it?
She hadn't exactly been tingling with interest
about how he had spent his time in the last
four years.

Addie gave Celia's cheek another pat as she

rose to her feet. 'I'll leave you now child, you need your sleep.'

Sleep was just a matter of closing her eyes.

CHAPTER THREE

THEY buried her grandfather in the little cemetery alongside the old wooden church that stood at the edge of the small town. By eleven o'clock it was over and the family waited about uncomfortably, careful not to leave too soon, while the old man's friends filed past offering awkward condolences, which none of them—apart from Addie—had any right to accept. Celia was conscious of a hard core of inner bitterness that lay like a stone in her chest and was surprised because she had thought she was past emotion of any kind.

In their well-cut, stylish blacks, the official party stood out like sore thumbs against the more restrained mourning and Sunday bests of most of the people who had arrived from hundreds of miles around to pay their last respects to Samuel Prescott. Elegant vultures, that's how her grandfather's friends must see them. In a flush of mortification Celia felt she had never liked her family less. It wasn't just the extravagantly fashionable clothes ... they could all have been garbed in the proverbial sack cloth and ashes and still managed to convey the unspoken disdain they felt towards 'the God-forsaken Outback'—and everyone in it.

Celia stood between Addie and Rick. They formed a separate trio on the other side of the

grave from the main party of official mourners—
an academic division. Even in Addie's classically
styled, navy silk dress, produced out of a musty
cupboard that morning and still reeking of
mothballs, Celia felt intrinsically part of them
and every bit as much an interloper—and
hypocrite. She fought the thought away, aching
for the whole thing to wind up so she could
escape the judgment of the eyes that tried not to
stare at her.

She was glad of Rick's presence. Grim, with
lines of strain showing around the grey eyes, he
looked formidable in his dark suit, but oddly
protective. Rick had remained with them instead
of joining his own family and Celia supposed it
was to give Addie moral support, but whatever
his reason, and in spite of her hostility, she
appreciated the gesture.

'I think we can leave now,' he murmured into
her ear and Celia nodded, relieved. She had hated
every moment from beginning to end—particularly the end.

She glanced across to the other group to signal
her mother they were ready to leave and
accidentatly caught Lucy's eye—no mean feat
considering the obliterating black straw structure
on Lucy's head. Her sister's version of funereal
headgear would have turned startled heads on
any racecourse. Lucy had been staring, only
waiting to catch Celia's attention before she
started moving out of the line-up towards them.

Not now, she didn't want to talk to any of them
now especially not Lucy. Celia made a soft
groaning noise and watched in dismay as Lucy

picked her way daintily across the unsettled earth in preposterously high heels.

'Celie darling! George told me you arrived last night—I was so sorry to have missed you. What a lovely surprise ... isn't it Rick?' she cooed huskily, flashing Rick a brilliant smile, and totally indifferent to time and place.

'Hello, Lucy,' Celia mumbled, aware of curious eyes trained on them. Lucy had never lacked drawing power.

Without any perceptible change in his grim expression Rick gave Lucy a curt nod. 'We'll see you all back at the homestead,' he said, very politely, and took Celia's arm while his eyes searched Addie out from a group that included his own family.

Lucy's smile faltered, then switched off with the abruptness of a light, making way for the pout. 'I suppose the same arrangements apply for the return trip?' The voice was as petulant as a thwarted child's.

'Yes, they do,' Rick agreed smoothly, 'unless your mother wants to offer you her place on the plane.'

'Not likely! Damn! It was a beastly drive.' Lucy's dark eyes narrowed. 'Nice to be some people ...'

Celia winced at her sister's slow, knowing smile that carried all manner of innuendo in its charming curve. She was about to snap, 'For God's sake take my seat,' when Rick gave her a little push and manoeuvred her away, leaving Lucy standing—furious at the prospect of another long hot drive and, Celia suspected, positively livid at Rick's quite deliberate lack of reaction to her.

The return flight to Mandarah was as silent as the flight into Banergee Hills, yet this time the silence seemed as vibratingly taut as a guitar string about to snap . . . or was she imagining it? Was she just being oversensitive to atmosphere? Something felt . . . was, different, Celia was sure of it. Her eyes chanced on Addie in the front seat beside Rick, glanced off the profile, then flipped back in a double take. Addie's earlier dead-pan calm was gone. She was almost visibly seething in some sort of feverish excitement. If it wasn't for the seat-belt strapping her into the seat, Celia had the feeling the old lady would simply take off on her own steam.

So the repressed emotions were finally surfacing in their own eccentric fashion, Celia thought pityingly, with a lurking half-fear that if her own were let loose Addie's wouldn't appear all that eccentric.

She was not the only one who had noticed the difference in the old lady. Eleanor shot Addie a curious look as Rick helped them all out of the plane. As usual, Addie ignored her, and Eleanor focused her attention on Rick. She beamed him a radiant smile—the original of Lucy's carbon copy. 'Thank you ever so much, Richard, you've been simply marvellous.' She placed a hand on Rick's arm in an intimate, ill-placed gesture and received a stony, 'Not at all, Eleanor,' in return.

Eleanor removed her hand smartly. The smile stayed in place just long enough to save face but it was not hard to tell she was furious. With a pathetically careless toss of her head, she moved on ahead of them, leading the way towards the lawns and homestead buildings.

Addie gave a malicious cackle.

'I'll come in for a drink, then head for home.' Rick sounded tired as he offered Addie his arm.

Celia walked alongside Addie, embarrassed for her mother marching resolutely in front and piqued with Rick for the gratuitous snub. Why did he have to be so damn high-handed about Eleanor's petty efforts to be attractive to all men? Rick knew Eleanor well enough to know she simply couldn't help herself, any more than Lucy. Being beautiful wasn't all it was cracked up to be, Celia decided sourly, sorry for both of them.

'I want you to stay—and you'll need to be there when the solicitor chap turns up,' Addie said casually to Rick.

'Why will I?' Rick demanded with sudden sharpness. And Celia wanted to know too.

'He'll be here around four. I decided we might as well get that will out of the way—that's what everybody is here for after all. I arranged to have him flown in from Sydney,' Addie rambled on, deliberately off point, and just when Celia thought she wasn't going to answer Rick's question, Addie threw him a peculiarly inscrutable look which she possibly meant to convey some profound message. 'Sam particularly wanted you to be there—that's why.' She didn't add 'so there', but it was that tone of voice.

'I see.' There was a very long pause. 'Very well, I'll stay,' Rick agreed tonelessly and sounded as if it was the last thing he wanted to do.

Celia didn't blame him for that, but what did he see? What had Rick concluded from Addie's cryptic comment? She frowned trying to puzzle it out in her head as they walked along in silence. Then just when they were crossing the lawns at the side of the main house, she saw it too. Like an answer to a frustrating crossword clue, it flashed in out of the blue and shocked the breath out of her. Grandfather had bequeathed Mandarah to Rick! Celia was as certain of it as if she had seen the will itself. The sudden riot inside her head made her feel weak. In the hall she muttered, 'I have a headache,' and shot off to her room.

Without a thought for Addie's delicate silk, Celia threw herself on the bed and blank-eyed stared up at the ceiling, eyes following the floral pattern of the old-fashioned cornices without really seeing them. What she saw was Rick Harland striding around her old home—the new owner of Mandarah—and without even having to buy it! Having it handed to him on a plate by a grateful old man. How could grandfather do it?

Well, why shouldn't he? It was his to leave, wasn't it? Celia demanded in belligerent despair, unaware that in her agitation she cried out the words aloud.

'What was whose to leave, dear?'

Celia jerked herself up into a sitting position. 'Oh, it's you.'

'Don't sound so pleased to see me,' Eleanor said peevishly, very obviously still smarting from Rick's snub.

'I'm sorry Eleanor, I didn't mean it to sound like that,' Celia said quickly, genuinely contrite and purposely calling her mother by name, which she usually tried to avoid. It never managed to roll off the tongue naturally, even if her mother did like it. She swung her legs down to the floor. 'I'm glad you've come,' she said and felt downright mean because she would have preferred to be alone. 'We haven't had a chance to talk yet, have we?' She smiled invitingly.

They had exchanged a few perfunctory comments before the flight that morning—and if Celia thought about it, perfunctory comments had been their regular means of communication for years.

Mollified, Eleanor smiled back, then wrinkled her nose delicately. 'That dress, darling . . . just the teeniest bit whiffy . . .'

'It stinks,' Celia agreed blandly as her mother eyed it critically.

'Hmm. Looks okay . . . amazing how styles come back. I remember Addie in it years ago.' Eleanor drifted soundlessly around the room, an incongruously elegant figure among the remnants of Celia's childhood. She touched things here and there, a brush on the cedar dressing table, the tattered one-eared bear on the window ledge. Celia watched her.

'It's a long time since I've been here,' Eleanor turned to her smiling, almost wistfully. 'After I married George, Sam didn't like me around much—it was all he could do to put up with the sight of me at Christmas.' She gave a self-deprecating little shrug.

What do you say to something like that? Celia asked herself with a surge of pity and said nothing. Her mother had stated no less than the truth.

Eleanor came to stand in front of her. 'I actually came in to say that I know how hard all this is for you, darling. I'm really very sorry. Sam meant a lot to you and you to him—particularly after Jim died.' She sat down on the bed beside Celia and fiddled nervously with the numerous rings on the finely boned fingers.

Involuntarily, Celia glanced down at her own, long firm fingers, devoid of any jewellery. Her hands, like the rest of her, were pure Prescott. Beside them her mother's looked like those of a child. Years ago Celia had been painfully sensitive about her height—and with Eleanor and Lucy as models of ideal womanhood, it wasn't all that surprising. She had grown out of her sensitivity but it took a long time to come to terms with her own very different attractiveness.

'You may find it hard to believe,' her mother continued to stare down at the rings, 'but I often envied you your love for this place—and this life.' She looked up, large, violet-blue eyes moist. 'I couldn't help hating it you know,' she said defensively. 'I just wasn't cut out for it. I hated it right from the beginning when Jim brought me here. God, how I hated it! The heat . . . the isolation—everything.' Her voice shook with the force of emotions the memories aroused. 'I never stopped being a stranger . . . it was hard on your father,' she added softly.

'Hard on you,' Celia said sympathetically.

Eleanor sighed. 'Fate can be very cruel,' she murmured more to herself than to Celia, then looked up. 'There was nothing to keep me here afterwards—after Jim died ... Lucy was already about to leave for Sydney, and you were at school. And you never really needed me, even when you were at home, did you?' The voice had an anxious, pleading tone as if, after all this time, Eleanor was asking Celia to confirm that she had done the right thing.

To her own, and possibly Eleanor's surprise, Celia put an arm around her mother's shoulder. They sat in silence for a while, sharing an awkward intimacy.

'You mustn't mind George.' Eleanor's thoughts had drifted on ahead. It was a familiar phrase. Celia had heard it often during the time she had lived in George's house. 'He's a good man at heart—and I'm happy,' her mother said simply. 'We suit each other. I can't really expect you to understand. I just wish that my marriage hadn't drawn us so far apart. Lucy never seemed to mind.'

The marriage had only been the last link in the chain of alienation which had begun years before George had ever come on the scene. All throughout her childhood Celia had never been part of the cosy, utterly feminine world that Lucy, four years older and cast in the same mould, had shared with Eleanor. Fashion, hairstyles and their mutual hankering for the bright lights had welded mother and older daughter together and left Celia on the outside, but it was water under the bridge now, and much

too late in their relationship to try and analyse the
whys and wherefores. Celia removed her arm
from Eleanor's shoulder.

'And what about you, darling? What are your
plans—are you going back to London?' Eleanor
asked, as if she had only just remembered that
Celia had been away.

'I'm not sure,' Celia said truthfully and
regretted that it sounded so evasive—almost a
snub.

Eleanor didn't press. She stood up, patting the
shining, almost jet black coil at the back of her
neck with the practised, elegant gesture of a
beautiful woman.

'I suppose we ought to get ready for lunch—
the others will be arriving shortly. Poor George
will be like a bear with a sore head after that
drive. I shall have my job cut out chucking him
under the chin—chins . . .' she laughed, enjoying
her little joke at her husband's expense. 'And
then Addie has lined up that solicitor for later—
dear me, what a day.'

'You knew? About the solicitor coming?' Celia
suppressed the surprise from her voice.

Eleanor arched a professionally defined eyebrow. 'Yes, of course. Didn't you? Addie told us
when she rang us in Sydney to tell us about Sam.
She told Beth and Julian too. Apparently Sam
wanted us all here together for the reading of the
will.' She allowed herself the smallest of frowns.
'What do you think that means?'

That he's lined up a colossal shock for us all!
Celia thought, grimly amused. 'I've no idea,' she
replied lightly, giving her mother a faint smile.

The road party was late back, tempers frayed to shreds. Celia took one look at her stepfather and braced herself for the worst. Predictably enough, lunch got off to an awful start.

George scowled up the table at Addie. 'I can't see why you didn't have the funeral in the city Adele—damned inconvenient having it here in the backwoods,' he said churlishly. 'Whoever heard of driving nearly two hundred and fifty kilometres just to bury a chap?'

They all stared in mild disbelief at his gaucheness while Addie looked positively dangerous. She finally unclamped her lips. 'It's usual to be buried where one has lived all one's life,' she replied acidly, but with marvellous self-restraint, and everybody seemed to breath a communal sigh of relief.

'What are you all staring at me like that for? I'm only saying what most of us are thinking,' George muttered, glowering at anyone who caught his eye. 'What the hell is the matter with everybody?'

'Nothing old chap,' Julian felt impelled to assure him hurriedly.

Eleanor stepped into the breach. 'Do try some of Mrs Gatley's ham, George,' she suggested placatingly. Her lovely eyes skimmed around the table and settled on her former sister-in-law, the only person attacking her plate with any show of appetite. 'Mrs Gatley has coped remarkably well with the catering, don't you think, Beth?'

Startled by the direct address, Beth lifted her head from her plate guiltily. 'What? Oh yes, yes she has. I don't know how she's managed with so many extra people in the house—and at such short notice,' she said very enthusiastically and darted her attention back to her food.

Celia picked at her plate uneasily, determined not to catch her mother's eye and be forced into some inane comment to fill the yawning gaps in the conversation.

'Don't talk rot, the pair of you!' Addie's voice was loaded with irritation. 'You've both lived here long enough in your time to know how property cooks manage. The reason Susan has coped is because we're always prepared for extra mouths to feed. You may have forgotten, but we don't have a corner shop to run to for fancy putty every time a visitor drops by.'

Lucy threw her head back and laughed immoderately. Julian sniggered at the cute, but quite deliberate mispronunciation of pâté, and even Celia felt a smile etching itself across her face. Cathing Rick's slow wink across the table she lowered her head quickly, annoyed that he was singling her out as some sort of ally in the discordant group.

'It'll be a blessed relief when this wretched place gets sold up, that's all I can say.' George came back into surly form and the light moment might not have existed. 'You're damn lucky I've got a mining company already interested in it. Lord only knows no one else in their right mind would want to be saddled with it. These oversized properties have had their day, if you ask me.' He glared around the table waiting to be challenged, and Celia held her breath, waiting for Addie's explosion.

When it didn't come she glanced up curiously
to see Addie smiling. The reason behind that
smug, secretive smile was not difficult to work
out. Celia risked a quick look at Rick. His face
showed no expression and reminded her of a
poker player who knows he's holding the winning
hand. Addie wasn't the only one anticipating
George Carr's comeuppance.

Oblivious to the intruding foot whenever he
opened his mouth, George grumbled on, keeping
up a non-stop flow of ill-humoured observations
throughout the meal. The only saving grace as far
as Celia was concerned was that no one got a
chance to start plying her with questions about
her own future plans. She wasn't expecting to
escape the family's curiosity indefinitely, but at
least George staved them off for just that little bit
longer. She sent a silent message of gratitude to
her brash, thoughtless stepfather as he sniped
about the lack of air-conditioning in 'the
wretched place', and was almost tempted to agree
with him.

Lunch ended with an abruptness that would
have given a hostess nightmares for a week. The
minute the girl from the kitchen arrived to clear
away, everybody rose *en masse* and practically
bolted out of the room. Celia took the opportunity
to escape outside. If she went to her room, it was
ten to one someone would turn up for an
unwelcome *tête-à-tête*.

Steering well clear of the part of verandah that
was directly outside the french windows of the
living room, she settled around the corner, with
every intention of sweating it out in the

breathless heat until the solicitor turned up. Her watch already showed a quarter to four. Another fifteen minutes—half an hour at the most and . . . why not face it? In another half hour the solicitor would be announcing to all and sundry that Rick Harland was the new owner of Mandarah and that would be that, Celia told herself with grim relish. Everybody could go home—furious and disappointed; George ranting about contesting the will—on Eleanor's behalf, of course; chartering planes with angry haste. Celia could picture it all—up to a point, then her imagination failed her. The part she couldn't visualise was where she herself fitted into that frantic picture.

Staying on at Mandarah was out of the question now, and so for that matter was going to Sydney to stay with Eleanor and George. The only real alternative was London, only that presented a small problem. She wished now she hadn't been quite so generous in handing over the remainder of her lease in the flat to Kel, the young artist who had moved into the spare room about two months ago. The move had been her idea and it had worked out well. She had enjoyed his eccentric companionship immensely and Kel had been typically Irish in the extravagance of his appreciation. 'You'll never regret this my girl, when I'm famous—not to say, rich, I'll remember my patroness.'

She was hardly that. Kel paid his rent and contributed what he could towards the housekeeping—not much, granted, but Celia believed in his very real talent and that made up for a lot.

Perhaps if she was quick enough she could make it back before Kel found someone else to share the rent. Her things were still there, waiting until she sent word where Kel was to send them. And, she thought, suddenly cheered, there was every possibility her job might still be available too. It was unlikely that Derek would have replaced her within a week. She would send a telegram to both of them to say she'd be back. When? If today was Wednesday ... Celia lost herself in calculation, and the footsteps coming along the blind side of the verandah were at the corner before she became aware of them. She lifted her head, composing her face into an icy mask of discouragement.

'I've been looking for you.' Rick flicked her a faint smile, loosening his tie as he came towards her. He hadn't taken off his jacket and Celia suspected that he had kept it on during lunch to annoy George and Julian who had emerged from their drive with sleeves rolled up and looking as if they had walked all the way.

'I came out here to be alone,' Celia said with asperity.

'And I came out here to talk to you,' Rick replied affably, but his eyes held a wariness at odds with the smoothness of his voice. He pulled up another wicker chair to the outdoor table, then hesitated, his hand on the back of the chair. 'I should have brought us out a drink. Shall I get something?' He looked at her questioningly, saw the sullen shake of her head, and settled himself into the chair.

It was no use wishing him away. 'Look, you've

been very kind about everything and I . . .' Celia attacked first.

'Don't you start on that!' Rick cut her off unceremoniously, the scathing emphasis an unmistakable reference to Eleanor's earlier display of gratitude.

Celia contemplated the stony face with its hard grey eyes. 'You can be very cruel, Rick Harland,' she said with quiet venom. 'It probably bucked your ego up no end to see Eleanor—and Lucy, playing their harmless little games. It wouldn't hurt to be . . . kinder.' She wasn't quite sure that was the word she wanted. She had in mind something like 'chivalrous'.

'I thought you were just saying how kind I am,' Rick caught her out deftly.

'Very funny. You know very well what I mean,' Celia snapped crossly.

'Yes, I do. And both your mother and sister should do me the courtesy of not playing me for a fool,' Rick retaliated with unexpected heat.

'They don't mean anything,' she rose to their defence. 'It's . . . it's just the way they are.'

Rick jerked up an angry eyebrow. 'Anything is forgivable if you're beautiful enough?' He gave a sour laugh. 'I don't buy that—they're a couple of very spoilt ladies and I didn't come out here to talk about them—fascinating as they find themselves—nor to hear you choke, telling me how kind I've been.'

'Then we've nothing to talk about as far as I know,' Celia said loftily. She edged her chair away from the table to get up.

'For God's sake, Celia, stop being so bloody

childish. I know you're mad at me—you haven't stopped being mad at me since you proposed to me and I turned you down—regrettably, rather abruptly—and that's what we're going to talk about at long last. So sit down. You're staying here if I have to tie you down to that chair.'

CHAPTER FOUR

RICK'S words caught her in the act of rising from the chair and froze her in position like someone in the childrens' game of Statues. She gaped at him in disbelief, then without any direction from her brain and without taking her eyes off his face, Celia lowered herself down again.

Every shade of red must have been searing over her face. It felt on fire as the sweeping rushes of anger and hatred followed hard on that first crushing assault of embarrassment. Her eyes sparked green fire. 'I wondered how long it would take you to dredge that up!' Celia spat the words out with scorching contempt. She gripped the edge of the table so rigidly her knuckles showed white but it didn't stop the shaking.

Her scorn glanced off Rick like a paper dart. He shrugged with maddening nonchalance. 'One of us had to,' he said reasonably. 'This stonewalling of yours has gone on long enough, Celia. We could have had this out on the plane yesterday, only . . .' Rick's mouth twisted into an acidic curve, 'the state you were in, you'd have leapt out in mid-air if I'd pushed it.'

Celia stared back murderously and Rick's expression hardened. 'I'm bringing it up now, because, I repeat, one of us had to, and since you've managed to avoid it—by avoiding me, for

four years, I might add—it's obviously up to me.
You've never given me a chance to explain why.'

'There's nothing to explain and I don't want to
sit . . .'

'Shut up! I'm sick of your knee-jerk reactions.
You're going to sit here and listen to what I have
to say.' Rick suddenly reached across the small
table and before Celia realised his intention,
unclamped her fingers from the table and closed
his hand over them.

Celia glowered sullenly but made no move to
wrench her hand away. After a moment Rick
seemed satisfied that she wasn't about to bolt for
it and relaxed his grip slightly. 'There are a few
things I'd like to explain to you, Celia—about
that time.' His eyes stayed on her face,
compelling her to hold his gaze. 'Why I reacted
as I did—I know I confused you, and hurt you
terribly . . .'

Something snapped inside her. Celia snatched
her hand back. The high crackling laugh that came
out of her mouth was a surprise to her— certainly
she had never heard it before. 'You can't have taken
me seriously! Good heavens Rick,' she chortled,
gasping for breath, as if he had just told her a very
funny joke. 'I was a child—a mere child,' she
trilled, way out of control. Part of her mind was
aghast, the other juggernauting determinedly on to
make a complete fool of her. 'There's nothing to
explain—I was a silly schoolgirl—infatuated I
admit and clutching at anything to thwart
George—anything! Nothing was further from my
mind than marrying you. I don't wonder you were
startled . . . I . . .'

He was watching her, face expressionless, but his eyes held a pained, humiliating kindness that ripped her pride to shreds. Why was Rick letting her go on like this ... tripping over the awful memories as she went. 'I don't wonder you were startled.' Hadn't she just said that? Celia snapped her mouth shut, tried to smile wryly and failed miserably because her bottom lip trembled so much. She dropped her eyes down to the table.

'You never were much of a liar, Celia,' Rick said softly. 'Even as a child, one hard look and you'd blurt out the truth in two seconds flat—it's too late to start practising now—particularly on me. I know you too well.'

Celia lifted her head, seizing at the sharp bolt of antagonism to bolster her pride. 'You knew a schoolgirl, Rick Harland—a schoolgirl of seventeen and she certainly isn't me—not any more; so don't tell me you know me—you don't. I'm not a child anymore,' she flung at him, labouring her point into the ground.

'Good,' Rick snapped with staccato shortness. 'Then perhaps we can talk like two adults about something that's very important to both of us.'

'Don't flatter yourself! It wasn't important to me then, and it certainly isn't ... Hello Addie!' Celia quite bellowed, looking past Rick's shoulder and smiling bright relief at the approaching Addie.

His back to Addie, Rick muttered an obscenity and scowled at the interruption.

'There you are, my dears,' Addie beamed at them, too obviously pleased to find them together. 'You'll melt out here, come inside. Old

Burgess has turned up—you probably missed hearing the plane over the other side.' Eyes glinting, Addie gave Celia a heavy-handed knowing smile. 'Sorry to interrupt.'

Celia served up a tight smile in return. 'You're not interrupting. We weren't discussing anything important.' She flashed Rick a look of defiant dislike as she jumped to her feet.

'I'll talk to you later,' Rick threatened in an undertone.

'Not if I can help it,' Celia returned just loud enough for Rick to hear and hurried after Addie.

George was still at it when they entered the living room. After what she had just been through the sight of her stepfather had never been so welcome. Sprawled in the middle of the large sofa at the back of the room, George was expounding on some remarkable business coup he had just pulled off. A glazed-eyed Julian sat trapped on one side, while on the other, a serene Eleanor paid no attention. Celia would have cheerfully traded places with either of them; alongside George would have been the safest place in the room. She gave him a quick smile as Addie marshalled her past.

Beth Lacey was staring into space in one of the arm chairs. She had changed into a light-coloured frock which didn't do much for her alarmingly increasing bulk, and she even less for the dress, despite its obvious expense and the right amount of restrained good taste. Lucy, still in her elegant black tunic, belted with a ton weight of silver metal, glanced up from the inspection of her long red nails to give Celia a hard suspicious stare, and looked very like a bad-tempered little blackbird in the centre of the oversized armchair.

Ignored by the lot of them, the elderly, thin man sat awkwardly behind the small mahogany table that had been opted into service as a desk for him. A number of chairs had been brought in from the dining room and arranged in front of the table in two rows, producing an effect of an impromptu schoolroom. Addie led Celia to the chairs and grasping her arm, yanked her down. 'We'll sit here—right in front,' she said. Her excitement was almost at fever pitch. She gave a quick glance behind and seemed satisfied. 'Start when you're ready, Paul,' she addressed the solicitor impatiently. Celia winced for the hapless man who couldn't possibly mistake Addie's meaning—start now and hurry up about it!

Paul Burgess looked up, thin face flushed pink, as if he hadn't quite yet recovered from being rushed from plane to desk without a pause for breath. 'Yes, well . . . yes, well . . .' he murmured looking at Addie reproachfully. He slipped incredibly long thin fingers into the flat leather document case on the table in front of him and drew out a suitably impressive looking folder.

'Isn't this exciting Rick?' Lucy giggled close behind. Celia stiffened.

She hadn't turned around when someone had taken the chair behind her, now she realised it had been Rick. He was virtually breathing down her neck, with her fool of a sister, impervious to all manner of snubs, beside him. His presence suddenly reminded Celia what their argument on the verandah had temporarily driven out of her mind: that Rick was a very interested party in this essentially family gathering. A very interested party, indeed, she thought bitterly and was glad that she was going to be spared the sight of his pleased face when the moment came.

'Yes, well . . . it seems that we are all here . . .' Mr Burgess' eyes took in his audience.

'Of course we're all here! Get on with it man!' George bellowed from the back of the room.

Mr Burgess looked pained and lowered his eyes. The prim, almost spinsterish voice started its soft drone, 'The last will and testament of Samuel John Prescott . . .'

There were bequests to staff . . . to friends . . . provision for Adele May Prescott for the duration of her life . . . Celia switched off. The words disposing of her grandfather's money became a blur, hypnotically soothing. She listened to them without taking them in. Then she felt Addie tense on the edge of her seat and involuntarily Celia tensed too. Glancing sideways, she met Addie's eyes, dancing wildly in a feverishly flushed face.

'. . . and my property Mandarah, and all buildings and stock that constitute this property I hereby bequeath jointly to my beloved grand-daughter Celia Elizabeth Prescott and to Richard James Harland . . . on condition . . .' The voice cut off theatrically. Celia gave an indrawn gasp. Mr Burgess looked up as if to ensure that he had their undivided attention, then apparently satis-fied with the shock on everybody's faces, dropped his eyes to the paper in his hand. Just behind her ear, Rick drew in a sharp breath that sounded like a hiss in the silence.

The blood rushed out of her face. Celia stared aghast at the unperturbed dried-up old man, screaming inside her head because she knew what was coming.

'. . . On condition . . .' he dragged out the words again, getting full measure out of his performance, 'that they agree to marry each other within one month of this day and that their marriage takes place no later than one month after that. If these conditions are met, the property Mandarah, will be assigned to them on the day of their marriage. In the event of these conditions not being acceptable to either party, the said property shall be put on the open market upon the expiration of one month from this day, and when sold the proceeds distributed equally amongst the following . . .'

Celia's mind went blank. She sat immobile, eyes pressed shut tightly. If she moved she would fall off the chair. The voice went on forever, and then finally there was nothing but a stunned silence.

Then George laughed—a long, loud, braying laugh that grated across the unnatural stillness. 'The old man was nuts!' he choked through the laugh that was perilously close to hysteria.

Celia opened her eyes experimentally, testing out her muscle control and found that it still worked. She also found she could still breathe and let the air escape out of her lungs in a slow painful shudder.

'Senile, that's what he was! Totally barmy!'

George tried to laugh again but ended up in a wheezy splutter.

Eyes flashing with angry triumph, Addie was on her feet. The parchment-like skin was bright pink and she was breathing hard, chest heaving as if she had just finished jogging around the home paddocks. 'Oh no, my man!' she hissed at George, 'Sam was no more senile than you are—he knew exactly what he was doing!'

He can't have! Celia yelled in silent agony and thought she had cried out aloud when Addie flung her a crazy flushed look. She turned away from it, hating the old lady with a surge of raging fury.

Across the space of the four feet or so that separated them, Celia met Mr Burgess's gaze. It held not a shred of curiosity nor surprise in it. Celia dropped her eyes, feeling as if layers of skin had just been peeled away, leaving her utterly exposed to ridicule, if not from the incurious solicitor, then from everyone else in the room.

Like persistent gnats, the voices buzzed around her ears, and all the time she was acutely aware of Rick, silent behind her. She fought the unbearable impulse to turn to him, too terrified of what she might see in his face.

Julian was saying 'But is it valid . . . legally, I mean . . . such a condition?'

'Of course it isn't!' George roared in answer. 'It can't be! Good Lord, the old chap forgot what century he was living in . . . he . . .'

'It's valid, yes . . . unusual, but quite valid. And since more than adequate bequests have been made to all present, there are really no

grounds for challenge under the recent Act. You
see, in nineteen eighty-one . . .' Mr Burgess'
threatened treatise on recent legislation was
snipped off by Beth's squeaky voice. 'Unusual?
It's positively medieval.'

'Who'd have thought the old boy so romantic?'
Lucy tried to sneer, not very successfully.

'I don't know why you're all getting so heated,'
Eleanor's sweet, reasonable voice drifted soothingly across the room. 'After all, it's unlikely that
Celia would agree to such a condition—or Rick
either. Mandarah will simply be sold at the end
of a month.' She spoke as if neither Celia nor
Rick were in the room at all. In fact, it seemed to
Celia that the two of them had somehow become
invisible.

And George laughed again. 'That's my gal!
You're not half as scatty as you make out, are
you? You're perfectly right, we . . .' he stopped
abruptly.

The chair scraped behind her. Celia heard Rick
cross the length of the long room and the door
slam. The silence he left behind was full of a new
edginess. Celia could sense the embarrassment
that had finally penetrated the family's communal
thick skin and knew she was now the focus of
their attention.

She felt eyes boring into her back as she sat
rigid, staring at nothing in particular, inanely
concentrating on the unnaturally loud ticking of
the clock on the mantelpiece. They were all
waiting for her to make the next move—to say
something. Even Addie, still on her feet, seemed
uncomfortable.

Celia had nothing to say to them. With ice-cold calm she rose from her seat, and holding her head high to avoid meeting anyone's eye, left the room with a painful show of dignity.

Outside in the hall, the calmness deserted her. For a moment the trembling was so bad she had to lean against the wall for support. After a while she felt she could rely on her feet to hold her up again and tried to work out where she wanted them to take her. She had to see Rick—had to explain that she had nothing to do with the preposterous will . . . that she hadn't persuaded Sam to make it in another bid to get him to marry her. Would he believe her? She doubted it, and doubted whether her nerves were up to a confrontation just yet.

As Celia dithered indecisively, the living-room door swung open and Addie charged out, invisible demons at her heels. The unnatural colour had gone from her face, leaving it a pasty white. She looked about a hundred. 'He's taking off! I saw him from the window going to the plane.' She made agitated fluttering movements with her hands in all directions at once. The only expression in her eyes was a kind of un-comprehending disbelief.

Celia turned on her. 'Having just sprung that on him, you can't be trying to tell me you're surprised! What did you expect him to do? Whisk out a ring from his pocket?' she yelled, shocking herself by her own vehemence. She wanted to pick up the old lady and shake her till her teeth rattled. 'It was a crazy thing to do—crazy and cruel. You knew it all along, didn't you?' she accused, her face contorted with hostility, and too upset to worry about the state Addie was in. Addie backed away, staring at her wildly. 'You knew it, Addie, I know you did!'

'Yes, I knew,' Addie admitted in a weak frightened voice. 'Sam and I discussed it for a long time . . .'

And Celia could see them in her mind's eye, two old people hatching their little surprise, unwittingly plotting her humiliation.

'It's just the surprise, Celie,' Addie rallied a little. 'Rick wants to marry you—it was Sam's way of getting you together again. Celie child, don't look at me like that . . .' she pleaded into Celia's furious face.

'He'd have done better to have minded his own business—and that goes for you too! Rick doesn't want to marry me, any more than I want to marry him—and if he does want Mandarah, he doesn't want it that badly,' she flung at the old woman, shocking what little was left of Addie's spirit completely out of her.

Addie seemed to crumble. Her face wrinkled over and for the first time ever, Celia saw tears gather in the aged grey eyes. She was appalled at the sight.

'Come on Addie, let me take you to your room . . . you need to lie down,' she said gruffly and gripped Addie's arm—not very gently—before the old lady fell down.

Addie allowed herself to be led to her room. 'It will turn out for the best yet, Celie; Sam was a wise man. You mustn't think he was an interfering old fool. It will turn out right . . .'

Addie kept saying, as if the words were a magic charm and if she repeated them enough they'd come true, but her voice didn't carry much conviction.

'Yes, as soon as George's mining company rips the place apart,' Celia muttered harshly, almost pushing Addie down on to the bed.

She couldn't stay—couldn't trust herself not to lash out in fury and humiliation at the crazy dry stick of a woman that had shrivelled up under her very eyes. Addie was in no condition for a verbal lashing. 'I'll look in on you later,' Celia said in a strained voice from the doorway, ignoring the pathetic appeal in the old lady's face.

'Excitement too much for the old girl?' Lucy smiled archly, not bothering to disguise the fact she had been eavesdropping outside the door. The incredibly dark blue eyes glittered with curiosity.

Celia shrugged non-committally. She might be furious with Addie, but discussing her with Lucy was another thing. 'I'm tired Lucy, leave me alone.' Celia tried to pass the determinedly unbudgeable little figure. Lucy didn't give an inch. 'She was so worked up at lunch I thought she'd burst—I wondered what she had up her sleeve, the wily old thing. She knew all about it of course and was having fits just waiting for that announcement—no wonder she's ready to pass out.' Lucy's eyes combed Celia's pinched face. 'You don't look too good yourself. Come to my room, I've got a bottle of whisky in there. You could do with a drink, to put it mildly,' Lucy offered, baiting the trap with a small dose of genuine concern. 'Do Celie, you've got to talk to someone and it might as well be me—you'll be too furious with Addie to say a civil word to her for days—and I don't blame you.' For all her self-absorption and tactlessness, Lucy was no slouch when it came to reading people. Celia's moment of indecision was her undoing. Lucy reached out a hand. 'Good girl. You'll feel better when you've got it off your chest.' And Celia found herself being raced along the passage, as if Lucy was intent on getting her out of sight before someone snatched her prize away.

Celia slumped into the gold velvet armchair in what was Lucy's old room. It still seemed full of Lucy—feminine and very pretty with just a hint of the gloss that Lucy would acquire when she left Mandarah. Impassively she watched her sister rustle about getting their drinks. 'There you are then,' Lucy smiled encouragingly, pushing the glass into Celia's hand.

'Thanks.' Celia took the glass and lifted it to her lips. She took a gulp, and gasped as the unfamiliar liquid seared down her throat, then grimaced with distaste.

'Don't knock it. It's the best whisky you can get—present from an admirer,' Lucy added, settling herself on the bed where, propped up on her elbow, she studied Celia with a patronising smile. Celia ventured another sip. This time the fiery taste had a peculiarly soothing effect.

Satisfied, Lucy took a sip of her own drink, eyeing Celia over the rim of the glass. Having got her sister where she wanted her, Lucy got straight to the point—her point. 'You should have seen Rick's face!'

Celia, thankful she hadn't, flinched at the crude launch-off.

'He went as white as a sheet—stunned, darling, stunned like a mullet.' Lucy mixed her similes with extravagance.

The direction that this irregular sisterly chat was going to take, stuck out a mile. 'It's hardly surprising he was angry,' Celia said steadily into her drink, avoiding Lucy's eyes. If she showed any sort of reaction Lucy would never let up.

'Angry? Who said anything about angry? I said stunned.'

Celia glanced up. 'What's the difference?' she asked, camouflaging her surprise that Rick hadn't looked furious, behind a front of careful indifference. She didn't doubt Lucy's interpretation of Rick's reaction for a moment. Her sister was not likely to have missed the smallest variation in his expression. If Lucy said he looked stunned, stunned he looked, but having just been done out of Mandarah, Celia would have expected that he'd look pretty angry too.

'A lot of difference, believe me.' Lips pursed into a speculative pout, Lucy contemplated Celia's guarded face for a drawn-out moment, then rearranged her lips into a faint smile. 'You are going to marry him, aren't you?' The inflection was barely interrogative.

Celia lowered her glass, carefully, because her hand was not very steady. She held Lucy's eyes. 'Don't be stupid, Lucy,' she said, quite pleasantly, holding back her shock.

Lucy arched an eyebrow. 'Stupid? Not at all.' Her lips curved into a hint of a sneer. 'You'd do it just to spite us—George particularly—and to get Mandarah, even if you didn't want Rick Harland—which you do. It's heaven-sent, the old idiot's will, isn't it?'

'I'm not staying to listen to this.' Celia put her glass down on the nearby dressing table with a restrained slam and got to her feet—slowly, so as not to give her sister an inkling of her agitation. 'You're letting your very active imagination run away with you, Lucy.' Her voice shook a little but otherwise there was nothing in it to give her away.

Lucy gave a tinkly laugh. 'Rick has always been your sensitive spot, hasn't he? You were always crazy about him—we all were at one time or another.' She laughed again. 'A female would have to be blind to be indifferent to Rick Harland—though God knows he can be beastly. Poor Eleanor got her comeuppance when she sent out feelers.' Lucy grinned with reminiscent relish. 'You were too young then to appreciate what went on.'

Halfway to the door Celia's mind focused in to what Lucy was saying. She swung around. 'You can't mean Mother? Rick?' she squeaked, and unthinkingly took a couple of steps back into the room.

Lucy gave the closest thing to a refined guffaw. 'Don't be such a baby! Of course Eleanor did a line for Rick after Dad died . . . why shouldn't she? Mind you, she didn't get very far,' Lucy added maliciously.

'But . . .' Celia found the idea appalling.

Tickled pink at the effect she had produced, Lucy grinned appreciatively. 'Why the horror, darling? After all, Eleanor was just in her mid-thirties when Dad died, and Rick was what . . . only about ten years younger. There's nothing so dreadful about that.'

'But she's always hated the Outback!' Celia blurted out.

It was Lucy's turn to look stunned. 'What on earth has that got to do with it?' Then the penny dropped. 'Marry him! Is that what you think she wanted to do?' Celia blushed furiously. 'Good grief, you really have come down in the last shower, haven't you?'

It certainly looked like it. How could anyone be so naïve . . .? Hot with silly embarrassment for the show of childishness, Celia made for the door. She'd had about as much of Lucy as she could take in one go. 'Thanks for the drink,' she tossed tersely over her shoulder.

'Something happened that Christmas, didn't it?' Lucy changed tack suddenly—and too casually, ignoring Celia's desperate lunge to the door.

Hand on the doorknob, Celia stood stock still. Walk out—now, she commanded herself—and turned around. 'That Christmas . . .? Which Christmas do you mean?' she reproduced Lucy's casualness tone for tone.

'You know exactly which one . . . *that* Christmas,' Lucy said in big, capital letters. 'Something did happen, I could tell from the way Rick came thundering up on that poor horse looking fit to kill. He'd gone to look for you by the river, and my guess is that he found you—and something happened—it must have, for Rick to have taken off in that plane of his like a bat out of hell—just like now . . .'

The heat in Celia's cheeks came in pulsating waves. She turned her face away abruptly from those lovely scrutinising eyes and stared blankly at the shrubs outside the window. Lucy had hit the raw spot with unnerving precision, but it was more than her life was worth to let her sister realise that.

'He was pretty shaken,' Lucy went on. 'There's not much I miss noticing when it comes to men,' she added, smugly.

The hot pounding in her cheeks had stopped. Celia looked away from the window into Lucy's watching eyes. She put together a pinched smile. 'I'm sure that particular talent comes in very handy in your busy life,' she said acidly, and instantly regretted stooping to cattiness to get back at Lucy.

The beautiful olive skin was obviously much thicker than it looked. Lucy could not have cared less. 'Yes, it certainly does,' she agreed cheerfully, 'you should see some of the creeps that hang around models.' She shuddered delicately.

'No thanks,' Celia said primly.

'You know,' Lucy went on conversationally, 'Eleanor and I could never work it out—your desperation to get away from Mandarah—particularly after all your tantrums about not wanting to go. You haven't seen much of Rick lately, have you?' She tossed in the question with wide-eyed innocence, and that was the last straw as far as Celia was concerned. She looked Lucy straight in the eye. If curiosity was a colour it would have to be that deep, violet-blue, she thought, and answered 'No' very steadily, then spoilt the effect by adding, with too much vehemence, 'Nor want to!' as she moved to the door.

'Celia!'

Something in the voice made Celia stop. She looked back into the room. Lucy was not smiling anymore. 'I don't know why you turned him down in the first place,' Lucy said, astonishingly, 'but nothing's going to stop you this time, is it?' Bitterness shaded the voice.

Celia felt her jaw dropping. 'This time . . .?' At the same instant, she thought: Lucy's jealous!

'Don't pretend Rick didn't ask you to marry him that Christmas—or that you haven't been kicking yourself ever since.' Lucy was angry, really angry. Celia was amazed. 'Anyone with half an eye can see that you're madly in love with him—the way you avoid looking at him half the time, and can't take your eyes off him the rest. And you practically vibrate when he's anywhere near you—oh yes, you'll marry him all right. You're crazy about him.'

White-faced, Celia found her voice. 'You're out of your mind!' she rasped and slammed out of the room.

CHAPTER FIVE

SHE couldn't lock her door. The key had gone missing years ago and had never been replaced. It had never mattered—until now, when Celia knew with dreadful certainty that if anyone came searching her out for one more ghastly *tête-à-tête*, she would have a nervous breakdown on the spot.

Leaning back against the door she eyed the carved wooden chest under the window and wondered whether she had enough strength left to drag it across the room without emptying it first. It was stacked full of her old books and toys and felt like lead before she got it across the door. She sank down on it, feeling an idiot for barricading herself in, but past caring; her mind was in total riot and the whisky wasn't helping. It seemed to have shot straight to her head instead of stomach and was beating out a throbbing tom-tom of pain somewhere behind her eyes adding to the fuzziness that had settled in hours ago . . . or was it days?

Celia got up with an effort and peeling off Addie's dress, still wafting up its years of mothballs, slipped between the ice-cold sheets. Damn Lucy, she muttered viciously and closed her eyes. Lucy's angry little face hovered in front of her closed lids with the persistence that was her sister's trade-mark, taunting her with that last incredible statement.

Love Rick Harland? After what had happened? The joke was certainly on Lucy. Head pounding, face burning, Celia tried to laugh. If only Lucy knew. She wouldn't be talking such rubbish about that Christmas—or anything else. No, she'd be laughing herself sick instead. Celia felt nauseous herself as the awful sequence of flashbacks started rearing up in her mind, just as they always did when she was at her most vulnerable and didn't have the strength to fight them.

She was home from school for good that Christmas and without a care in the world, apart from the mixed up emotions towards Rick Harland who she had known all her life. Crazy emotions—thrilling one moment, disconcerting the next. She flushed madly every time Rick's gently amused gaze rested on her when he picked her up at Mt Isa that last time. She was in love— as chaotically and painfully as only a seventeen- year-old can be, but would have died a hundred horrible deaths before letting anyone prise her secret out of her.

The family had gathered for Christmas—even Lucy, all condescension and charm, had breezed in from New York, or wherever she had just finished her photographic assignment, with her latest boyfriend in tow. Mandarah buzzed like a beehive in full swing and Celia had been truly happy, counting the hours to Rick's next visit from the family property which he managed for his father. It was nearly two hundred miles away, but a neighbour in Outback terms; he came often and secretly she let herself hope it was in order to see her.

Looking back, Celia supposed it had all been a bit too good to last. On Christmas Eve, George dropped his bombshell. 'It's time to get you away from this God-forsaken Outback. You can't rot here forever. We're taking you back to Sydney to live with your mother and me,' he stated baldly and was totally unmoved by her tears, arguments or tantrums.

She hadn't believed it could happen—not until her grandfather, and even Addie, incomprehensibly sided with George and then the bottom fell out of her world—or so it had seemed when Celia galloped off from the homestead that afternoon heading for the river to get away from them all—Grandfather included.

No one ever came near the particular stretch of river about seven miles from the homestead which she had earmarked from childhood as her own special place. She threw off her clothes, plunged in, and threshed about like a demented fish, swimming off the pent-up anger and despair.

Rick had known where to find her. When he turned up, Celia was sitting on the bank in her knickers, drying off, her shirt draped loosely around her shoulders. Too upset to even think of covering up, she poured out her misery to him as he sat beside her. In the end, she broke down and howled like a child and Rick drew her against him and held her close—like a child. At first.

Afterwards, Celia could never really remember how that kiss came about. Everything else about it, however, was branded into her brain—every little detail from the first soft, comforting touch of Rick's lips, through their gathering urgency, to the unfamiliar violent surge of response that his hungry mouth drew from her. She clung to him, her unclothed breasts bruising against the roughness of his heavy-duty cotton shirt, and then tingling with a frightening pleasure as Rick's hand started its gentle stroking over them.

Almost mindless, she abandoned herself to that kiss—a far cry from the brotherly pecks that Rick had planted on her cheeks over the years. She wanted it to go on forever but pulled away, breathless, and insanely happy. 'Marry me Rick!' she cried. 'Please marry me, then George won't be able to take me away.'

Rick had snatched his hand from her heaving breast as if it had burnt him.

The look in his eyes scared the wits out of her. In a mass of confusion Celia drew back from the glittering anger without understanding it, knowing only that she had caused it. And then as if it wasn't bad enough already, her little secret blurted itself out. 'Please Rick, I love you,' and she could have died.

Rick stared in a sort of savage despair, then pressed his eyes shut as if he couldn't bear to look at her. When he opened them again, the anger had gone out of them. They looked curiously dull. 'Get dressed Celia, you're not enough of a child anymore to be sitting around topless,' he muttered, voice harsh and uneven, and if he had struck her she could not have been more shocked nor humiliated.

Rick had ridden off then, and was gone when she finally returned to the house hours later. They had not met again—not until a few days ago when she found him waiting for her at Mt Isa, just like all those other times. Celia knew he had wanted to see her. He had made all those trips to Sydney, calling at George's house—and never finding her at home. There had been letters too, that she had returned unopened, and each time Celia felt she had scored a victory—a singularly sour little victory, denying Rick the opportunity to settle his conscience on the point of manners. His rejection of her had been pretty crude and it was a fair assumption that he wanted the chance to soften the blow. He should have saved himself the trouble; nothing that he might have said could have made her hate him less.

Sometimes Celia was almost surprised by the continuing intensity of her feelings, and the bitterness that had become so insidiously obsessive—always eating away at her. In her more rational moments she disliked herself for giving in to it for so long and wasting so much mental energy on something so unproductive as hate.

She had been hopelessly young and inexperienced—then. Wasn't it time to put the episode behind her? Why couldn't she laugh it away? It was funny enough—an infatuated seventeen-year-old throwing herself at a thirty-year-old man and expecting to be taken seriously. Unsurprisingly, Rick had rejected her and that was that—or should have been. Seeing Rick again had renewed all the humiliation. She couldn't

look him in the eye without feeling that he was
laughing at her. No, that was not true. Celia
remembered the look in his eyes; Rick was sorry
for her and that was a hundred times worse.

And what was he thinking now? That she'd
had a hand in cooking up the terms of Sam's
preposterous will? Rick had flown off without
taking his things and that meant he'd be coming
back. She would get up soon and try to find him.

It had been light when Celia closed her eyes
and it was light when she opened them again—
but a different kind of light ... harsher ...
sharper. Morning; and not only morning, but
well into it. Eyes fixed unseeingly on the ceiling,
Celia lay listening to the familiar sounds that
were so intrinsically Mandarah. Thousands of
homesick miles away in London she used to
evoke the same sounds from memory ... voices
calling out in the stables ... the faint whinnying
of horses ... the piercingly raucous screech of a
crow flying past. This morning they jarred on her
nerves like so many off-key notes.

Her eyes drifted down to the chest against the
door and stayed there as the appalling events of
the previous day came back in snatches like
images from a nightmare. Making no effort to
fight them, Celia lay still until they finally trailed
off into a wearying nothingness, then very calmly
got out of bed and pushed the chest back to its
position under the window.

Later, showered and dressed in an old pair of
jeans and T-shirt selected from the still-wearable
leftovers in the wardrobe, she sat on the chest
and gazed across at the stables, putting off the

inevitable moment when she would have to go
out and face Rick. She could do it, she told
herself firmly, all she needed was a little more
time to get her head together—to rehearse her
lines well enough to come through the encounter
with some semblance of composure. Just at this
moment she was not ready for Rick.

All the time Celia had been staring at the
stables without her mind taking in what she was
seeing. Suddenly, she gave a little exclamation.
Reprieve was just a couple of hundred yards away!
She jumped off the chest and darted to the
wardrobe, and had the riding boots half on when
the tap on the door came. It was only one hard
rap and she didn't have time to react before the
door swung open.

'You're up. Good.' The tall, skinny old lady
could have passed for Addie's sister; even the
voice had the same crackly quality. 'Yes, it's only
me,' she said drily as Celia's face relaxed visibly
at the sight of the housekeeper. Susan eyed the
boots askance. 'Not before you've had breakfast,
I hope.'

Celia smiled brightly, over-reacting in her
relief that it hadn't been Rick after all. 'Just a
short ride, Susan, I promise . . . I'm not hungry
anyway.' The way her stomach felt, Celia
doubted she would ever feel like eating again.

'Hmm.' Susan studied her, frowning. 'You do
look peaky, perhaps a ride isn't such a bad idea
. . . just make sure you're back for lunch though,
my girl.'

'Yes, I will.' Celia would have promised
anything. 'Is Addie . . .?'

'I've just looked in on her. She's all right—asleep again. I made her go back to bed. She shouldn't have got up in the first place after yesterday's high jinks.' Susan cocked her head to one side like a bright-eyed old parrot. 'Took the wind right out of her—and not just her, I'll wager.' She smiled a worn-out, knowing smile. Celia ignored it.

'Is . . . where is everybody?' She changed the question around in the nick of time.

'If you mean Rick Harland,' this time Susan's smile carried a hint of wryness, 'he was around earlier this morning . . . I don't know where he is now.' The shrewd eyes stayed on Celia's face. There was not much that went on in the homestead that escaped the old housekeeper, and what she inadvertently missed, she would pick up from Addie anyway. The old ladies had been friends for too long for secrets.

Celia turned away from the silent scrutiny. 'I'll be back for lunch. Thank you, Susan,' she said, dismissively.

It was water off a duck's back. 'Make sure you are,' Susan muttered, with cheerful belligerence, not the least put out by Celia's resort to high-handedness.

Avoiding the main part of the house Celia hurried—sneaked?—down the short passage that led to the side door of the house. Rounding the corner, she pulled up short. Another step would have tripped her over Julian Lacey, on his hands and knees on the floor beside a small, but rather lovely old cottage dresser against the wall. Her uncle sprang to his feet, face beetroot, looking for

all the world like an overgrown schoolboy caught
at something he shoudn't be doing.

'Good heavens, Julian, what are you doing?
Have you dropped something?' Celia smiled,
intrigued by the surprising display of guilt.

'Oh . . . ah . . . good morning Celia . . . yes, I
. . . that is no . . .' he broke off helplessly,
grinning like mad.

Celia contemplated him quizzically, watching
the beetroot flush weave its way up the high
forehead and into the scalp, disarranging Julian's
carefully co-ordinated colour scheme. After the
previous day's mourning, he was back to his
regulation muted greys and blues—from the
carefully casual gear to his silvery hair, baby blue
eyes, and faintly grey skin tones. The dark red of
his face clashed horribly with everything.

'What on earth have you been up to?' she
persisted, curiosity aroused, and determined to
prise his guilty secret out of him. With his inane
grin growing more awful every second, Julian
dodged about in front of the dresser, a hand
behind him fumbling on its polished surface.
Celia noticed the tape measure an instant before
his hand found it and tried to scrunch it up out of
sight. She frowned. 'What have you . . .?' she
started, and then knew. 'You've been measuring
it! You've been measuring this dresser haven't
you?'

'Well, I thought . . .'

'You thought you'd lay claim to it, that's what
you thought!' Celia was so angry her voice shook.

'No need to take on so, Celia . . . after all, it's
not . . .'

'Not mine?' she finished off for him. 'Is that what you were about to remind me?'

'I wasn't doing any harm.' Her uncle switched to defensive self-righteousness. 'I happen to know a chap who'd be very interested in it and . . .'

'And you can't wait to sell it to him! And I suppose Beth is running around the house sticking sold stickers on all the paintings around the place?' Uncontrollable tears of rage made her eyes sting.

Julian gaped, swallowed a number of times and looked away. Never very vocal at the best of times, he was rendered utterly speechless by her exhibition of emotional fury.

'You just can't wait, can you? You're . . . you're abominable!' Celia flung at him and stormed off, astounded by her irrational fit of temper. Another moment and she would have actually hit her slightly dandified, but basically harmless, uncle. Her nerves were in a worse state than she thought.

It wasn't just Julian. She had only caught him in the act, but the others were probably roaming around the enormous house, marking out their spoils at this very moment. And why shouldn't they? What gave her the right to hate them for it? She had no special claim on Mandarah. Not unless . . . and that was out of the question.

It was Celia's first ride for ages but she was in no mood to enjoy it. All the way to her stretch of river she rode the uncomplaining Elly as if both their lives depended on getting to the river in record time. The humid heat swirled around her

like a damp mist; in minutes, the clingy material
of the T-shirt stuck like a clammy second skin
and she was vaguely aware of the wet sheen on
the animal's back. Celia dug her knees into the
horse's sides regardless and didn't let up until
the tops of the clump of stumpy trees became
visible over the slight slope that hid the river
from view.

At the sight of the leafy patch against the
horizon she finally slowed them down and they
took the slope at a fast, as opposed to furious,
gallop. At the bottom of the slope she saw the
familiar curve of water, the group of scraggly
trees and in the same instant, Rick, sitting on the
ground, his back against the trunk of one of the
trees.

Celia's first instict was to jerk the reins and
head Elly back up the slope as fast as her legs
could carry them. Rick had seen them—having
probably heard them from a mile away, and was
already drawing himself to his feet. What was the
point in turning back now? She might as well
have it out with him here with no one walking in
on the encounter.

She guided Elly down the slope and dismounted
under the meagre shade of the trees where Rick's
stallion stood calmly chewing at the few tufts of
long grass. With her stomach starting to churn,
Celia fiddled with the saddle, stalling for time.

'I knew you'd turn up here sooner or later,'
Rick said behind her. 'Here, let me . . .'

Celia moved aside and Rick took off the saddle,
putting it on the ground near his own. He ran a
hand along Elly's flank, then wiped the wet hand

across his jeans in a pointed, silent censure.

'I ... we ... had a bit of a gallop,' Celia muttered defensively.

Rick looked her up and down slowly, his eyes coming to rest on the damp patch of material between her breasts. 'You look as if you changed places with Elly along the way. Come and sit down,' he invited politely, and Celia felt like a reluctant guest cornered by her host and with no means of escape.

She sat down on the grassy patch on the bank, wondering how it was all going to begin. Rick lowered himself down beside her and both of them stared down at the water. 'I didn't know—about the will . . .' Celia surprised herself because she had no idea she was about to speak. 'I had nothing to do with it.'

'I know that,' Rick said casually.

'Oh. Well, that's all right then. I thought you might have . . .' Celia gave a small embarrassed laugh and shut up quickly.

'You thought what?'

'Nothing.'

'That I thought you'd somehow engineered it with Sam?'

It was exactly what she had thought. Celia flushed, aware Rick was studying her profile. She lifted a hand to her hair and twirled a long red strand nervously between her fingers, blocking her face from view.

'Damn it, I wish you'd look at me once in a while instead of always turning away,' Rick grasped her wrist and brought her hand down hard on to the ground between them.

'What do you think you're doing?' she yelped angrily.

'I said I wanted you to look at me.'

She glared mutinously at him. 'Why should I?'

'So that I can see your eyes—that's the only way I can tell what's going on inside that head of yours'' Rick answered with irritation. 'We've got a lot of talking to do—and spare me the mandatory protests, I'm not in the mood for them.' Rick barked as Celia opened her mouth. She snapped it shut. 'We're going to talk about that will.'

'I've already told you I had nothing to do with the crazy thing!' she burst out.

Rick's mouth jerked upwards. 'So you think it's crazy, do you?' he asked with an edge to his voice that made it sound more threatening than if he had shouted the question.

Celia nodded wildly. 'Of course I do and so do you.' She tried to read the expression in Rick's eyes. 'Don't you?' she added, uncertainly.

'No, I don't, so I'll thank you not to put words into my mouth. I happen to think it's quite a reasonable will, all things considered.'

Reasonable? What was he getting at? Lucy had said Rick had been stunned—like a mullet. You don't look stunned by something reasonable. 'That's not what I heard,' she returned with an attempt at bravado.

The grip around her wrist tightened. 'And just what did you hear?'

She shrugged, not quite off-handedly. 'That you were . . . rather surprised.'

Rick released a harsh laugh. 'If that's the best your sister could come up with she's slipping. I

was more than surprised. Sam's terms set me on
my ear as much as everybody else, but that
doesn't mean the whole thing's crazy.'

Celia looked at him doubtfully, then incredu-
lously. 'You can't be suggesting . . .' The words
were too outlandish to say aloud.

'That we get married?' Rick finished for her.
'Yes I am.'

If her mind had been functioning properly
Celia would have burst out laughing. She might
yet—after the shock had passed.

'Don't turn away from me, Celia.' Rick edged
closer, the top of his arm touching hers, skin
against bare skin. She tensed, but could not have
moved to save her life. 'You said you loved me
. . . once.' The husky voice was right at her ear.
'And I wanted to tell you . . .'

'How dare you bring that up—now . . .?' she
exploded without warning, her hair swishing
against Rick's face as she swung to him. 'You
can't stop humiliating me, can you?'

Rick winced, his face a tight, angry white. After
a moment the colour came back. He said through
clenched teeth, 'That was the last thing I
intended,' and held her down by the wrist as she
tried to get to her feet. Celia sat down again, rigid
with hostility.

'My sense of timing appears to be out. I apologise,' Rick said stiffly. 'The suggestion still stands,
but I'll rephrase it to make it more palatable to
you: if you marry me, you'd get Mandarah.'

'And so would you!' Celia hurled back. 'And
isn't that what you're after since Grandfather
turned the tables on you?'

Rick drew in a harsh breath and released her wrist with such force that her hand was virtually flung into her lap. 'Just explain what you mean by that,' he hissed at her, his face menancingly close.

His reaction had shaken her and her voice rather squeaked. 'All I meant was that you probably thought Grandfather was going to leave Mandarah to you outright.'

Rick's mouth twisted—half sneer, half smile, both bitter. 'So that's what your tiny mind had deduced . . . I should have guessed.' The short ugly sound was nowhere near a laugh. 'And you'd have had me snatching up my inheritance . . . just like that?' he asked, too quietly, with venomous restraint.

The conversation suddenly seemed to be full of hidden traps yawning open all over the place. Celia measured her words out carefully. 'You always said you wanted your own property one day . . . and now that your brother is keen to take over the management of your family's property, well . . .' Celia trailed off with a shrug. She tried not to scramble to her feet too hurriedly, but Rick was starting to frighten her. 'Why didn't he leave it to Addie and be done with it?' she cried out in frustration. 'That's who Mandarah really belongs to.'

Rick's jaw dropped perceptibly in either real or feigned astonishment. 'You can't still seriously think that? Good God, you crazy idiot, I believe you do,' he laughed sourly. 'You seem to have overlooked that the admirable Addie is at least seventy-four—or doesn't that count?'

'That doesn't make her decrepit!' Celia shouted at him, irrationally taking the comment on Addie's age as a personal affront. 'And I would have helped her. I would have stayed on here and . . . and managed the place.' Hands on hips, she glared down at him.

'Oh, of course, I'd forgotten.' Rick's face contorted into a sneer. 'With your vast experience there'd be nothing to it—managing the men, the stock, the markets, exports,' he taunted, his eyes raging. 'After all, what's managing a couple of hundred thousand hectares after managing the hanging of a couple of dozen paintings on a wall? Obviously a piece of cake.'

She would have hit him only instinct told her Rick would hit back. 'I had a very responsible job, Rick Harland and I was very good at it— everybody said so!' She tossed modesty to the wind.

In one swift movement, Rick was on his feet, towering over her, dangerously close. 'I bet you were,' he jeered softly, 'and I don't doubt your very satisfied clients thought so, too.'

She frowned, puzzled, trying to hit on a meaning to the words that wasn't the awful one on the surface.

'You want me to spell it out, do you?' Rick took a step forward and like a partner in some impromptu dance, Celia took a step back. 'Shall I spell out the name of Kel McCarthy for a start? Surprised?' Rick grinned savagely into her face, and Celia took another hasty step backwards and hit the trunk of the tree with her back. 'You didn't know I was in London two months ago, did you?' He tilted his head sideways as if to get another angle on her aghast face. Celia shook her head dumbly—not in answer to the question, but in sheer speechless disbelief at what Rick was implying.

'Yes, I dropped by,' Rick said casually. 'Sam told me he thought from your letters that you wanted to come home at last . . . and I thought that meant you'd got yourself together and we could finally talk about things. Well, we were wrong—Sam and I. Weren't we? He didn't know about your Irish Picasso. You managed to keep that bit nice and quiet didn't you?'

'You've been spying on me!'

'Let's say I've been taking a keen interest in your affairs . . . that's the right word, isn't it?'

Celia raised her hands to lash out wildly at his chest, his face—or both, but Rick's fingers snapped over her wrists in mid-air, and brought them down roughly to her sides. He smiled dangerously. 'I don't fancy my face scratched to pieces.'

'You're hurting me!' Celia's eyes smarted with pain. Rick tightened the grip, determined, almost desperately to hurt her.

'And did you model for your live-in boyfriend?' he asked with mock politeness, making it sound as if he was asking after her health. The icy splinters of rage in his eyes would have stabbed her dead if it had been possible. 'Surely, you sat for him as well?'

As well? She knew what Rick meant and hated him.

'And what if I did?' she retaliated with a

sneering flourish. Yes, she had sat for Kel, but not in the way Rick meant. Kel had done a strange, enigmatic portrait of her shortly after he had moved in. 'It'll be worth a mint, one of these days, Celia my love,' he had said, laughingly, and she believed him—not because of the light-hearted boast, but because she genuinely believed in his very real talent. If she hadn't believed in that, she would not have helped him out by suggesting he move in to share the flat with her. Any explanation would be wasted on Rick. The likes of Rick Harland would never understand that it was possible to share a roof with a man and not be sexually involved.

Rick's eyes drifted insolently over her breasts and came back to her flushed face. 'And what about your other arty-crafty friends? Did you model for them too?' Like a dog with an old bone, he couldn't let it alone.

'You're out of your mind, Rick Harland,' she said with weary contempt. The innuendoes sickened her and all she wanted was to get away from him. Celia tried to tug herself out of the painful grip.

Rick took another step and closed the gap between them. 'Am I?' His breath was hot as it brushed her cheek.

In a wild moment of panic, Celia twisted her head from side to side. She opened her clenched lips a fraction. 'No!'

Rick's mouth found its mark and the fraction was all it needed to prise her lips apart with a force that wrenched the breath out of her. Rick let go her wrists, and pulling her away from the tree, made a savage band around her with his arms, moulding her against the hard lines of his body while his mouth pushed and rammed as if he hated her.

The violent heat kept pouring into her mouth until, incredibly, it started answering the angry demand with a fierceness and hunger of its own. Her mind, some part of it at least, was fully aware of what she was doing, but there wasn't anything it could do to stop it, or the surge of patently sexual desire that raced through her. Celia trembled with sudden violence as Rick made a deep groaning sound in his throat. At that moment the tempo of the kiss changed. Their mouths stayed locked, but probed with a new gentleness that did nothing to ease the throbbing inside her that was working itself into a frenzied crescendo.

Rick cupped her head with his hands, lacing his fingers through her hair, holding her head back as his mouth meandered down the arch of her throat in tormentingly tender exploration. Celia was making breathless whispering noises and suddenly heard herself. It was then reality zoomed back into unsteady focus. With her hands somehow already on his shoulders, she pushed him away. It was the last thing Rick was expecting.

The sudden shove caught him off-guard and almost off-balance. He looked startled, but that lasted only an instant. Her chest still heaving for air, and heart thumping overtime, Celia stared at him as if she had never seen him before, while Rick's eyes combed her face, examining it pore by pore.

They locked eyes at last and Rick smiled—a curious smile that was little more than an upward tilt of one corner of his mouth, yet managed to convey . . . what? The word 'satisfaction' floated into her thoughts and all the black humiliation from the back of her mind sprang forward. She had done it again—made a complete fool of herself. Every nerve in her body had screamed out her vulnerability to his touch . . . her crazy desire for him. It was a thousand times worse than when she had been seventeen. No wonder Rick looked pleased with himself. Was he waiting for her to blurt out that she loved him as well . . .? Just to add the finishing touch to the mortifying scenario. Celia pushed past him and dashed, stumbling as she went, towards the horses.

'Celia!' Rick cried out, shocked, angry, she couldn't distinguish. He caught up with her in a stride, and grabbing her by the arm, swung her roughly about to face him. Celia did not attempt to struggle. 'Leave me alone, Rick, hasn't your vanity been satisfied enough?' she said bitterly, her face a cold, white mask.

A sudden shadow passed over his features. 'Oh my God.' The frustration did not sound as if it was directed at her.

Celia said wearily. 'I'd like to go back now. If you don't mind,' she added with stinging courtesy.

Rick opened his mouth, closed it again and gave a jerky shake of his head, all without taking his eyes off her. She stared him out, and he released her without another word and went to saddle up the horse for her.

CHAPTER SIX

IGNORING Rick's outstretched hand, Celia mounted unaided. She didn't look around once yet could feel his eyes boring into her back as she headed in the direction of the homestead. Rick was very close behind; she didn't need to turn around to confirm it because his presence was as tangible as if they were still locked in each other's arms, their mouths deep in the continuation of something that had started a long time ago.

With nauseating certainty Celia knew she had been waiting for that kiss—for four years to be precise. In vivid mental replay she felt Rick's exploring mouth plumbing the depths of her own and hated herself for having wanted him as she had never before wanted any man; and hated Rick too, for being able to kindle the spark inside her.

No other man had done that; and there had been men interested in her—some persistent to the point of irritation. They had all lacked something she could not put into words—other than they left her cold.

Caroline, her boss's daughter, and Celia's closest friend in London, would throw up her hands in a great show of despair. 'But who are you waiting for Celia? The knight on the white charger? He doesn't exist you know, and it's not . . . well, not natural to be so distant and . . . cool

towards the poor chaps beating a path to your
door.'

Cool? Frigid, was the word that Caroline
delicately left unspoken. Celia might have been
tempted to think that was true if she hadn't had
the memory of how she had felt in Rick Harland's
arms all that time ago; but as close as their
friendship was, Celia balked at telling Caroline
about that, because it would have meant telling
her about Rick—no knight on a white charger—
an opportunist on a black stallion was more apt.
Well might he be prepared to marry her now with
Mandarah at stake.

For a brief moment Celia felt consumed by a
burning hatred for Mandarah, then as quickly as
it had flared, the feeling died, leaving a dull
misery in its place. Mandarah had always been
home, whether she was there physically or not,
and she loved it. How would she ever be able to
train herself never to think of it as home again?

If you really want to keep it that badly—the
small insidious voice inside her head tempted—
why not agree to marry him? Being Rick
Harland's wife would not be a hardship ... Celia
felt the pressure of Rick's body against her, all
over again. 'No!' she called out, horrified at
where the tumbling thoughts were leading her. A
business arrangement then ... the voice went on
seductively. She made an inarticulate sound into
the hot air rushing past her face and urged Elly
on with a jab of her knees, keeping up the pace
right through the home paddocks and into the
mounting yard.

She dismounted at a run, tossing the reins at a

slightly startled stablehand as he went by. Rick was too close behind her and Celia felt rattled. In her mixed-up mental state she simply couldn't trust herself alone with him; the safest place was amongst the family. Celia almost ran into the house as Rick came cantering into the yard.

She stood outside the door to the living room for a moment or two, catching her breath and trying to tidy her hair, which she suspected must look as if she had put her finger in a socket. There was a buzz of indistinguishable voices but she wasn't fussy as to who was in there. Anyone would do as a protective barrier if Rick followed her in.

Celia flung open the door. The action had the effect of scissoring the conversation in mid-air. She took a few steps into the hushed room, then stopped, a foolish little smile on her face, almost expecting a burst of applause from her audience. Her eyes took them in at a sweep and they all stared back—except Addie who continued her gaze out of the window. She wasn't thinking very straight because otherwise she would have recognised the blond man immediately. As it was she stared, frowning her puzzlement while she ransacked her brain for a name to attach to the face.

'Hi, Celia.' Mike Johnson rose from the armchair and came towards her, teeth glistening in the suntanned face. Something about her expression must have disconcerted him; he stopped mid-way across the room, letting the outstretched hand drop to his side.

Celia swung to George 'What is he doing here . . .?'

Mike continued the smile without showing quite as many teeth; his eyes were wary but it took more than rudeness to put him off balance. 'Why, I told you on the plane, Celia, that I'd be dropping by to inspect a property. Of course I didn't realise you'd be here . . . you could have knocked me over with a feather when George told me.'

Celia could have knocked him over full stop. The negotiator . . . George's rambling about the mining company, it was coming together . . . clanging into place.

'We've been having a family conference, Celia,' Lucy smiled with delicate malice. 'Mike's been tossing some figures around—about Mandarah that is. Luckily he has a calculator—you wouldn't believe how enormous the figures are.'

Celia swallowed hard. There was a searing dryness in her throat. 'Is that true?' she asked George in an unnaturally calm voice while her heart seemed to have stopped beating underneath the skimpy perspiration-drenched T-shirt.

George opened his mouth, but Eleanor edged into the pause. 'Have you been riding, darling? Why don't you freshen up then come and join us? Susan will be announcing lunch soon,' Eleanor said in her sweetest oil-over-troubled-waters voice.

'Shut up, Nora!' George didn't bother to glance at his wife. His angry eyes hadn't left Celia's face from the moment she burst into the room. 'Yes, we have been discussing what

Mandarah will fetch,' he said tersely, 'and I don't know why you're acting so put out about it. I asked Mike to come here today because there's no sense in wasting time when we can have everything sewn up by the end of the month that your insane grandfather specified in that outrageous thing he called his will. It's sound business to get the ball rolling as soon as possible. There's a lot of money involved, in case it's slipped your mind.' His voice rose and temper hung by a thread. The red of his face darkened as he glared, waiting for Celia to challenge his arrangements. Everybody else seemed to be waiting too.

Very slowly, Celia let her eyes range over her family. Eleanor was fiddling uneasily with her rings. Lucy, openly enjoying the turn of events, raised a sardonic eyebrow as their eyes met. Beth and Julian sat like a stage couple depicting nonchalance, and wrapped up in their pretence that all this had nothing to do with them, avoided meeting her gaze. Mike Johnson had the look of a man no longer sure of his ground—or his sale.

There was a slight movement from Addie as she turned from the window. Celia met the old lady's bleak look and the decision made itself. 'I want him out of the house,' she said at last, very evenly, her eyes still on Addie. Something flickered over the old face before Celia turned to address Mike. 'I assume that Cessna on the strip is yours and I suggest you round up your pilot and go back where you came from. I'm sorry if you've been inconvenienced,' she added with cold civility.

'Now look here, Celia,' Mike protested, rising anger sweeping a pink tinge over the tan.

'Leave her to me.' George took a step towards her.

Celia held her ground. 'I mean it George,' she said stonily.

'Is that so?' George sneered, jowly cheeks convoluting into rolls of animosity. 'Then let me remind you that you're in no position to mean anything—you're talking rubbish, my girl. It's not up to you to order anybody out of this house because unless . . .' he broke off, eyes somewhere past her shoulder, and as everybody stared towards the door, Mike Johnson seemed to draw himself up an inch and Celia knew that Rick was standing behind her.

'Don't let me interrupt. You were saying, George . . .' Rick's voice was chilling in its icy politeness.

George recovered himself with a scowl. 'I was saying,' he recommenced furiously, 'that unless the farcical marriage goes through, Celia has no more right to this place than the rest of the family—and can't just take it upon herself to order anyone out—and that goes for you too!' Hot and red, he threw down the gauntlet with bellicose bravado.

Celia did not move as Rick's arm wound around her shoulder. The room was very silent. She looked fixedly at a point on the back wall above everybody's heads.

'I'm afraid you're mistaken, George,' Rick corrected, so pleasantly it was menacing. 'Celia and I shall be getting married as soon as it can be arranged, so you see, Celia has every right to do as she pleases about Mandarah. And, I might add, I take exception to the term "farcical", and suggest you refrain from using it again in our presence.' The arm tightened around her shoulder.

It was fortunate it was there to hold her up because Celia had started to tremble. She wondered why she should react that way when she felt quite calm and so unsurprised.

'I don't believe it!' George was first off the mark.

Celia felt Rick's shoulder lift against her in a dismissive shrug. 'That's your problem,' he remarked coolly.

'Heavens, Celia, is this true?' Eleanor asked in a faint squeak, for once her social graces deserting her.

Looking past her mother's astounded face, Celia met Addie's expectant eyes. 'Yes, it's true,' she said in a firm, clear voice.

'I don't believe it!' George repeated, eyes bulging in something dangerously close to a fit. 'When was all this supposed to have happened anyway? You've hardly seen . . .'

'That's not really your business. Now if you'll excuse us . . .' Rick cut him off with barbed courtesy, 'Celia and I still have a few things to discuss.' Rick gave a nod to the room at large rather than any one in particular and propelled her to the door.

A few things to discuss? The outrageous understatement took Celia's breath away. 'The performance is over, you can remove your arm now,' she told him tersely as soon as they were in the hall.

'Shut up,' Rick returned with the same civility he'd used on George and the arm stayed put all the way down the main corridor, the shorter passage out of the house and across the yard. Celia felt like a prisoner being marched off to her cell, the arm as effective as any handcuffs.

It finally came off just inside the door of the lounge of the Manager's residence, but seemed to have left an imprint. Celia was still conscious of a heavy warmth around her shoulders although Rick was on the other side of the room at the drinks cabinet. 'Sit down,' he ordered, rather than invited.

She chose to remain standing until Rick came over with her drink, then feeling she had made some sort of indeterminate point, sat down and watched him return to the cabinet and pick up his own drink. With his back resting against the cabinet, Rick regarded her silently, his face unreadable. Then he lifted his glass in a salute. 'To us,' he said lightly, and she couldn't tell whether he was mocking or not. There was a tension in his body, a certain stiffness around the broad shoulders under the cotton shirt, that told her Rick was not quite as casual as he was trying to make out—and that made two of them.

Celia took a slow sip, congratulating herself on her calmness. Shock. Any moment, reality would set in and knock her off her feet, but in the meantime she was glad of the interim feeling of tenuous control.

'It will be strictly a business arrangement, of course,' she said briskly, needing to say something, and saw Rick's eyebrow shoot upwards.

'That wasn't what Sam intended, and certainly not what I have in mind,' Rick said, affably, but the underlying note of intransigence didn't escape her.

Celia did not know why she should have felt the small spasm of shock. It was only to be expected that Rick would try that on. 'Well, it's what I had in mind,' she snapped.

'Was it?'

Celia examined her glass, as intently as if it was the most fascinating thing in the world, while her mind swung into action, working out how best to handle this turn of events. She was angry, but on guard. The marriage—her version—was too important now, to risk antagonising Rick just at the moment. She needed him. 'Look,' she started, with an excess of reasonableness. 'When I said "Yes", I meant yes to a business arrangement in which we'd both get what we want—Mandarah.' She managed to keep the voice steady, but couldn't do the same with her hand and had to bring up the other hand to help hold the glass.

'And I meant a marriage in the truest sense of the word . . . a marriage in which I get a wife, not a business partner.' Rick moved towards her. Celia backed deeper into the chair at his approach and felt a fool. Rick did not look as if he was about to attack her. She dropped her eyes to the glass, not sure what he might find in their green depths.

Rick grasped her chin firmly and tilted her face up. She met his eyes reluctantly. 'Down there by the river I didn't get the feeling you'd find the idea of being my wife unappealing,' he said softly.

In a flurry of anger, Celia swatted his hand away. 'That's not fair! It's got nothing to do with it . . . it was just . . .' she shrugged jerkily.

'Sexual attraction?' Rick prompted mockingly.

She had more pride than to bluster a denial of something so excruciatingly obvious. 'It's hardly a basis for a proper marriage, if that's what you're after,' she muttered sulkily.

'It *is* what I'm after—a proper marriage, as you put it. And I'll make do with the sexual attraction—for a start.' Rick smiled, but only with his lips. 'I mean it, Celia. If you can't envisage sharing my bed . . . bearing my children, and everything else that being a wife entails, then you had better go straight back in there,' he tossed his head in the direction of the main house, 'and tell them you've changed your mind. Your stepfather and no doubt the rest of them will be too relieved to be annoyed by a bit of capriciousness—a lady's prerogative, and all that.' The arrogant casualness, whether genuine, or a put on job, gave the impression that Rick himself did not care less one way or the other. Celia knew better: Rick wanted Mandarah.

'You can't have it all your own way. You want this property as much as I do, and, since the only way you're going to get it is by marrying me, that gives me an equal right to set terms,' Celia pointed out—with admirable restraint, she thought.

'Don't be too sure about that,' Rick advised tightly, walking away from her. He poured

himself another drink and stayed on that side of
the room. 'You've changed your mind then?
That's fine by me, but you'd better go and set
their minds at rest.'

He was bluffing—he had to be. Yet . . .
conscious of a sliver of doubt, Celia contemplated
him uneasily.

'What are you waiting for?'

She lowered her gaze to his dusty riding boots
without answering. Call his bluff—now. Get up
and start walking out, she ordered herself, and
might as well have been glued into the chair—she
couldn't do it. 'You're taking advantage of me . . .
under the circumstances . . .' she said uncertainly.

'Advantage? Advantage!' Rick swooped the
word up with heavy-handed astonishment. Celia
looked startled. 'And when, pray tell me, have I
taken advantage of you? Was it four years ago
when a confused, vulnerable and very beautiful
seventeen-year-old threw herself at me? Was it
this morning by the river when you led me to
believe you wanted me to make love to you—then
turned on me as if I had leapt out of the trees to
rape you?' The muscles of Rick's face were seized
into knots of anger. His eyes lashed her
contemptuously as she backed deeper into the
chair. 'Or was it back there in front of your
family, when I stepped in to cut off George's so-
called negotiations with your Yankee friend
before he sold off everything you love without a
qualm? You could have said "no" then—and got
your own back for all the advantages you're so
convinced I've taken of you.'

Rick's body exuded a terrible anger. He was breathing hard and the clenched fist at his side frightened her more than a little. She couldn't meet his eyes. 'I . . . didn't know your terms,' she mumbled into her drink.

'Well, you know them now, so make up your mind,' Rick barked, offering her a mockery of a choice. 'And you've got about five minutes left to decide whether you want to accept them.'

'Five minutes?' A time limit for the most important decision of her life? Celia could not believe it.

Rick smiled without humour. 'Yes, five minutes—if you're lucky, because any moment now, your very inquisitive mother, not to mention sister, will have recovered from their shock and will be ferreting us out to talk wedding.'

'Wedding?' Celia squeaked like a parrot who could only reproduce the last couple of words it heard.

'Wedding,' Rick repeated sourly. 'It's likely to be of more interest to them than marriage. And as for that, if there's to be a marriage there'll be a wedding—I'm not sneaking off to a Registry Office for any three-minute whirl through the formalities. There'll be church and families—yours and mine, and the rest of it. Small and quiet, but a wedding. Yes or no, Celia?'

The picture rose in her mind and sharpened until she could see it all in perfect detail—the conventional wedding. And she could stop it now, with one word. 'And I suppose you'd like me to trail down the aisle in white, complete with veil and orange blossoms?' she taunted, shakily, rocked by a tremor of panic. The 'no' had got lost somewhere between her brain and her mouth, and whatever the words, what she had actually just said was 'yes'.

Rick looked at her unblinkingly as if he was turning over the picture she had just presented, in his mind. The sharpened light in his eyes told her he had decoded her words. 'Yes, I would like that very much,' he answered huskily. 'But orange blossoms are out of season and as for white . . .' he twisted out a sardonic smile, 'under the circumstances, I'll leave that to your discretion.'

Her supposed affair with Kel! Celia flared red, choking back the angry denial. He didn't deserve it.

'Sorry,' Rick said—with too easy penitence. 'And about what I said by the river too . . . your past is not my business.'

'Any more than yours is mine?' she retaliated heatedly.

She knew all about Rick's past. The Outback, enormous as it was, could have been the smallest village when it came to knowing about your neighbour's affairs—literally. Rick had been no monk and Celia had no reason to think he had changed his ways during the time she had been away. She recognised the hot spurt of emotion as plain old-fashioned jealousy and, to her humiliation, so did Rick.

He grinned wickedly. '*Touché*. We won't mention it again, will we?' In a change of voice he said briskly, 'I'll get on to Burgess to organise a special licence for us—we can easily be married within a fortnight.'

Celia gave an involuntary gasp. 'That's too soon!'

'Why wait?' Rick smiled indulgently. 'We can have it all over and done with and be back here by the end of the month.'

'But Sam's only just died. Doesn't anybody care about that? It's not decent.'

'Celia, Sam would approve, really he would,' Rick assured her gently. 'And I'm not talking about fanfares and trumpets but a quiet family wedding. There's no reason to put it off.'

Any resemblance to George Carr is not coincidental, Celia thought bitterly. There wasn't much to distinguish one from the other when it came to their eagerness to lay hands on Mandarah. She lifted a churlish shoulder. 'Yes, why not?'

Rick looked annoyed by her tone and she waited for him to snipe back. He must have thought better of it. His face cleared—or rather he cleared it carefully and his voice took on a very deliberate pleasantness. But he overlooked his hands which were clenched into tight balls. 'What I suggest is that you return to Sydney with the family, so Eleanor can get a start on arrangements. I'll have to stay on here until the last minute. With a push I'll probably just make it down in time to sign the papers and turn up at the church.' He smiled ruefully.

'Don't strain yourself on my account.' The anger was sudden and overwhelming. Celia was shaking with it. Having got her to agree to what he wanted, Rick was now going to bundle her off to Sydney and collect her on the day of the wedding like some parcel—gift-wrapped in white, at the *poste restante*—or the church in this case.

Rick reached down, plucked the barely touched drink out of her hand and placed it on the side table. He took both her hands and drew her to her feet. They stood very close—too close. Celia backed away like a nervous filly.

Rick pulled her closer until she was standing against him, their bodies touching. She held her breath, not moving as Rick cupped her face with both hands. 'It can work, Celia ... if you don't fight me.'

She opened her mouth to protest that since he had laid down the ground rules she wouldn't have much chance to fight him, but his lips descended softly and the protest died unvoiced, as his mouth expertly manipulated her into a sort of mindless acquiescence.

'Are we interrupting?' Eleanor's voice tinkled, a trifle self-consciously, from the doorway.

Rick released Celia's mouth unhurriedly and took his hands away from her face. 'Not at all Eleanor ... we've been expecting you—and you too, Lucy, haven't we, Celia?' he said urbanely and gave them the first real smile that Celia could remember him lavishing on either of them.

Eleanor's eyes fluttered over them, a tiny frown drawing her brows together as if she had trouble adjusting to what, to all intents and purposes, must have looked like a picture of the conventional happy couple. Lucy's eyes just held suspicion.

'If you're sure we're not interrupting ...'
Eleanor repeated diffidently.

'I imagine you'll have a lot to discuss,' Rick
smiled disarmingly.

Eleanor, only too ready and willing to be
disarmed, returned him one of her more
spectacular smiles. 'Well, if there's going to be a
wedding ...'

'There certainly is!' Rick laughed.

Celia read smugness into the laugh. And why
shouldn't Rick be feeling smug? He had them all
where he wanted. She had capitulated with barely
token resistence; Eleanor was ready to eat out of
his hand, and he'd find some way of getting
around the rest of them in no time.

Rick caught her hand in his. His fingers traced
teasing patterns into her palm. Celia looked up at
him and his mouth curved. There was some
message in his eyes she couldn't quite decipher.
Was he telling her this was her last chance to
recant? Or was he warning her against it? She
turned away—straight into Lucy's watching eyes,
gleaming with suspicion. Her sister for one, was
not entirely taken in by the appealing charade in
front of her. 'You will be my bridesmaid, won't
you, Lucy?' Celia asked suddenly and enjoyed a
childish triumph as the sceptical smirk was wiped
off Lucy's face.

Lucy made an inarticulate rejoinder that didn't
sound very gracious and Rick chuckled.

'George still in the living room?' He addressed
Eleanor, who nodded. 'Good, I want to talk to
him—and to Burgess if he's still around. Addie
said he wasn't due to fly out until this evening.'

He focused the full beam of his attention on
Eleanor. 'Would you be able to organise a small
wedding for us within a fortnight, Eleanor? Celia
and I want to get married as soon as the licence
comes through. I know it'll be a bit of a rush
but ...' he appealed charmingly, and Eleanor
melted visibly under their eyes. Rick Harland
could be very charming—when he chose. 'We
were rather hoping for Saturday week,' he
suggested, smoothly.

'Saturday week? Yes, I think so ... yes, of
course I can.' Eleanor's willingness to please was
almost pathetic and Celia disliked Rick for his
manipulation of her mother—whom he did not
like at all. It was probably just as well that
Eleanor was too absorbed in being attractive to
see through him.

'Great.' Rick smiled. 'I'll leave you to it then.'
He planted a careless kiss on Celia's cheek and
disappeared cheerfully out the door.

'That's what's known as a turn-up for the
books.' Lucy's eyes had followed Rick out of the
room. 'Rick Harland oozing charm and
bonhomie—towards us, no less, Eleanor.' The
thread of bitterness wove noticeably through
Lucy's artificial jocularity.

'Don't be so childish, Lucy,' Eleanor said
waspishly. 'I'm very happy for you, darling,' she
said to Celia, brushing her lips softly against
Celia's cheek. 'It is a surprise, of course ... but a
very nice one I'm sure. Oh dear!' she murmured
as she drew away.

'What is it now?' Lucy asked irritably.

'I forgot to congratulate Richard—it simply

didn't occur to me . . .'

Lucy laughed gratingly. 'I don't think he noticed, Mother. He was too busy conning you into organising his wedding practically overnight,' she said with a burst of peevish insight, and laying the stress on 'mother' to annoy Eleanor.

Celia's heart sank at the prospect of the next week and a half being spent in their bickering company.

CHAPTER SEVEN

'SMILE everybody ... that's it ... beeeautiful. Yes, that's great ...' The elegant sprite of a photographer clicked with demonic zeal, capturing them from every conceivable angle outside the small bluestone church. The happy wedding party. Wrong, wrong, Celia thought miserably and smiled harder. The smile felt taped up at the corners it had been there so long.

When the artistic little whirlwind had squeezed out the last smiles they were free to head back to the house. George had gone overboard and hired an awful white Rolls Royce, reeking of ostentation, for the bridal car—presumably so he could ride in more discreet style in his own Silver Phantom. Throughout the short drive Rick held her hand so tightly it was starting to turn numb, but he didn't say anything and Celia was grateful for that. If he had murmured something as trite as 'Well, Mrs Harland,' she would have screeched.

She stole a glance at his profile which looked as solemn as if it had been carved from stone. Outside the church Rick had smiled as hard as the rest of them and had looked pretty genuine— but then so had she, so that was not much of an indication of his feelings.

When was the last time they'd spoken—apart from exchanging vows? Amazingly they had not

stuck in her throat, but they hardly constituted
conversation. Celia worked back through the fog
in her mind. It must have been two days ago
when Rick came to the house for dinner. His
parents had been there, as well as his brother
with his very pregnant wife—all so delighted that
Celia felt an absolute heel and only hoped Rick
felt worse. If the Harlands were surprised at
having a wedding sprung on them at such short
notice, they kept it to themselves. The will, as if
by prearrangement, had tactfully not been
mentioned and Celia had no way of knowing
whether Rick had told his family of the bizarre
background to the forthcoming marriage.

There had been no opportunity to ask him
because they had not had one private moment
together. Later, it occurred to her Rick must have
wanted it that way and was annoyed she felt
disappointed. What had she expected? That he
whisk her away somewhere and coo sweet
nothings into her ear?

Ransacking her brains, Celia was hard pressed
to remember if they had said anything more than
'hello' and 'goodbye' since she left Mandarah a
week and a half ago, and looking at him now, she
wondered what on earth they were going to talk
about for the rest of their lives—when they had
finished hurling recriminations at each other.

Rick turned suddenly and smiled into her face.
It was a warm, lingering smile that reached right
into the depths of his eyes. For some inane reason
Celia blushed furiously, then quivered like jelly
when his lips touched her mouth in a soft kiss.
Another second and she might have started

returning the kiss. Might have. The car pulled up at the porch of George's house and Rick released her mouth. Celia didn't know whether she was glad or sorry.

Rick had wanted a wedding and Eleanor had made sure he got one; there were toasts, and cake-cutting, and restrained speeches—all supervised by a George who was positively skittish with *bonhomie* and a beaming smile that put Addie's in the shade. He acted as if the wedding had been his very own idea and had been like that ever since returning from Mandarah. Rick had obviously succeeded in putting something over on him—and the rest of them. Considering their initial reaction, no one could blame her for being cynical; they all looked too pleased for words and the Harlands' quite genuine pleasure seemed pale by comparison.

Celia kept on smiling mechanically through Eleanor's elegantly orchestrated production. Everyone told her she looked radiant whereas she felt like a battery-operated doll going through her paces, and not even the knowledge that she had secured Mandarah's safety could fend off the wild inner panic that she had done something she was going to regret. The champagne helped, each glass going some way in numbing the panic. The more she drank, the more it helped, so Celia made sure her glass was never empty—surreptiously at first, like a closet alcholic, and then it simply didn't matter who noticed. She laughed and talked a lot until Rick told her, pointedly, it was time to get ready to leave.

'Nervous, darling?' Lucy smiled coyly on the

way upstairs to change. 'You've been putting away the champagne at a remarkable rate. It's George's best French, granted, but . . .'

'I wasn't aware that anyone was counting,' Celia muttered, needled by guilt.

'Rick was,' Lucy returned with snide relish. 'I don't wonder . . . brides are not supposed to get drunk on their wedding night.' Lucy followed her into the bedroom and like a good bridesmaid undid the back fastenings of Celia's dress. 'He wasn't looking too pleased a moment ago . . .'

Celia stepped out of the simple ankle-length ivory silk and flung it in a heap on the bed. 'For God's sake, leave off, Lucy!' They might have been embarking on one of their teenage squabbles, with Lucy as always, intentionally goading Celia into losing her temper. 'Don't be mean to me, Lucy . . . please . . . not today,' she appealed wearily. She didn't need Lucy to tell her she had been overdoing the champagne—nor that Rick and everybody else would have noticed.

Celia slipped quickly into the sleeveless pale blue crêpe tunic and felt better just for having got off the bridal dress. She never wanted to see it again.

'You should really go for a deeper blue you know,' Lucy murmured, momentarily distracted. 'The pale looks better with colouring like mine . . .' She ran a hand over her own ice-blue silk. 'Anyway, why the miseries?' She returned to her main subject unmercifully. 'You should be the happiest girl in the world, to coin a phrase . . . you've just landed everything you've ever wanted—Rick Harland *and* Mandarah, though sometimes, I wonder which comes first with you.'

Lucy's was a rare talent—real insight coupled with refined malice, if not downright cruelty. Celia could not cope with it. She turned her back on her sister and began picking the flowers out of her hair. She had done Rick out of the veil but despite her protestations, hadn't escaped the bridal blossoms Eleanor and the hairdresser had insisted were a necessary substitute. Celia tossed them down uncaringly on to the dressing table and ran a comb roughly through the casually engineered waves. She was annoyed to find she could not loosen the hair back into its usual slight curves, and that the fragrance of the frangipanis persisted to waft about the strands.

'I reek like a florist shop,' she groaned, peering into the mirror. She stared, half-fascinated into her own flushed face. The eyes danced about crazily and she peered closer, thinking it was some distortion of the light—and got the same result. Drunk, she told herself tartly; she was drunk and looked it.

'Where's the honeymoon?' Lucy asked curiously.

Celia turned away from the mirror in disgust. 'No idea,' she replied off-handedly. Given a choice she would have preferred to leave the city and fly home as soon as possible, but Rick hadn't offered her any choice. It was only one of the topics they had not got around to discussing and she didn't even know whether he intended to pursue the charade to the final irony of a honeymoon at all.

Celia picked up her handbag and moved to the door. 'Thanks for being bridesmaid,' she said shortly, meeting her sister's eyes for a brief moment.

'Wouldn't have missed it for the world, darling ...' Lucy's arch little smile broadened into a grin. 'Good luck ... Something tells me you're going to need it.'

Celia sighed and went downstairs to tell Rick she was ready to leave.

There was the last minute whirl of farewells, smiles and kisses. If she hadn't known the circumstances, Celia might have believed their good wishes were sincere. Lord only knew Lucy was right; she needed all the good wishes she could get, but it stung to realise they seemed to know it, too. George was particularly demonstrative, and at the last minute, full of magnanimity and champagne, insisted his own chauffeur drive them away in his own silver Rolls.

Grateful for small mercies, Celia was relieved they would not be arriving at their destination looking like the traditional first-night honeymooners. 'Where are we going?' she asked in the car, aware of an unease in her stomach which might have been the result of too much champagne.

'To the hotel where I've been staying. I've booked us a suite for a couple of days before we head off.'

'Where to?'

'The Barrier Reef Islands ... we can hire a boat and do a bit of cruising ... if that's all right with you.' Rick said, anxiously, and Celia was seized with resentment at the tone. It was a little

late to sound anxious when he hadn't seen fit to
check with her before he made his arrangements.
She didn't answer and Rick gave her a sharp
look. 'I thought since you're just back from
overseas you'd prefer somewhere local ... we can
go abroad for a while later if you like,' he offered,
the slightest edge in his voice.

As far as Celia was concerned he could not
have chosen worse. The last thing she wanted
was to be part and parcel of the honeymoon
brigade on the islands. And trapped on a boat
with Rick ...? She'd rather take her chances with
a school of sharks. 'I'd have rather gone back to
Mandarah, but it doesn't seem to matter what I
want, does it since I was not consulted?'

She heard the faint cluck of Rick's tongue and
was pleased he was annoyed. After that ill-
humoured exchange, they stayed silent until the
car drew up in front of the hotel. 'Here we are
then,' Rick said with forced cheerfulness, gripping her hand as if he expected her to make a
dash for it. The thought did cross her mind.

The hotel was of the typical multi-storey
luxury variety—travertine marble, and mirrors,
and an excess of glass. The enormous suite was in
predictable, and very expensive good taste, all
neutral beiges and off-whites that would have
received an instant seal of approval from Eleanor,
and driven Julian into transports of ecstasy. The
paintings looked like originals and the view from
the sixteenth floor was breathtaking.

Celia slid open the glass doors and stepped out
on to the balcony while Rick attended to the
porter who had brought up her suitcase. It was

not very late and the night air hung like a warm cloud. In spite of the warmth, Celia shivered. She gazed across the glittering fairyland picking out the lights of the bridge and the Opera House and wished desperately she was back in the soft, enveloping darkness that lay over Mandarah, where the only sparkling lights were the stars in a jet-black outback sky. She sighed wistfully, then nearly jumped out of her skin as Rick's hands encircled her waist from behind.

'It's beautiful, isn't it?' he murmured.

'Yes,' she agreed tonelessly and tried not to squirm.

'And I haven't told you yet how very beautiful you looked today . . .' His lips brushed the hair away from the side of her neck and touched the skin warmly. 'How very beautiful you are . . .' he breathed huskily into her neck as his hands slid over her stomach, the palms exerting a gentle circular pressure.

Celia drew in her breath. The blue crêpe fabric was too thin a barrier between her flesh and the heavy warmth of Rick's hands. The combined sensation of the relentless hands and the exploring mouth nuzzling her neck just below the earlobe was exquisitely unbearable. 'Don't Rick,' she pleaded in alarm, grappling with his fingers.

The clasp tightened. 'Don't make it hard for me Celia. I've waited a long time for this.' Rick drew her back against the length of his body. Celia made a stifled moaning noise and let her head fall back on to his shoulder, her resistance crumbling. Nothing would have been easier than to drift mindlessly into the sensual whirlpool the pressure of his touch was creating for her to fall into—if there hadn't been the hard sharp voice inside her head telling her she was just part of the deal—that she had sold herself for a large tract of harsh outback countryside, and if she succumbed as easily as this she would never be able to face herself. Rick's hand's moved rhythmically upwards to her breasts.

Celia jerked herself straight and broke out of the clasp. 'Didn't I see some champagne in the ice bucket? she sang out, quite shrilly in the attempt to sound casual and shot past him into the room.

She found she was shaking as she snatched up the bottle. She needed another drink more than she realised. It was very expensive champagne but the vilest vinegar would have done just as well—anything to anaesthetise the tumultuous emotions into some sort of numbness.

Rick turned slowly and stepped back into the room. Tanned skin glowing bronze above the whiteness of his formal shirt, he looked incredibly handsome and her stomach gave an uncontrollable lurch as if his hands were still lingering over its curves. Never mind what her mind was telling her, her body was crying out another story: she wanted Rick—badly. The desire washing over her in tormenting waves made her feel weak.

As he came towards her Celia held out the bottle at arm's length to prevent him coming too close. Rick met her eyes and read her transparent ploy only too easily. He was angry. The dull, flat smouldering in his eyes set off quivers of alarm and she dropped her eyes. Without a word Rick took the bottle from her hand. Celia waited for a snide comment that she had already drunk too much. None came, and that made her even more nervous. She smiled a little to relieve her own tension as Rick removed the cork with a flick of the wrist and very deliberately—with an ironic ceremoniousness, filled one of the crystal flutes on the silver tray. The other stayed accusingly empty.

'Aren't you having any?' Celia asked, too brightly.

Rick held out the filled glass to her with a sardonic smile. She wanted to refuse it—maybe would have refused it if it hadn't been for that mocking expression on his face. Defiantly, she seized the glass out of his hand and took a long gulp. The bubbles tickled her nose and, nerves shot, Celia giggled and recklessly took another long gulp that finished the glass. 'It's delicious— do have some,' she invited gaily, hating herself— and Rick, for watching her with that cold detachment. She heard the falsetto laugh trill around the room and realised it must be coming from her own mouth.

Rick turned his back on her and walked through the connecting doorway into the main bedroom, Celia supposed it was. She watched him move out of sight—angrily, then refilled her glass with a flourish and drained it hurriedly, afraid that if she let herself come to her senses even for a second, she would do something even more stupid—like dissolve into tears. And if she started crying now, she would never stop.

She sank down into the suffocatingly soft

comfort of the over-stuffed armchair and went on sipping with grim determination. She could hear Rick moving about in the next room and it struck her as very, very funny that she should be polishing off a bottle of champagne alone on her wedding night. Celia laughed softly and drank a little more, finding that each sip of the tart golden liquid fuzzied the edges of her mind into a more bearable blur. She didn't notice Rick had returned until the glass was lifted out of her hand. Rick slammed it down on the tray. The noise produced a sharp stab of pain in her head. Celia winced and made a mumble of protest.

'Come on, you're going to bed.' Rick gripped her by both arms and hauled her roughly out of the chair.

Her body felt a deadweight and her feet seemed to have suddenly become so tired they had trouble in supporting her. Teetering unsteadily, Celia looked down at them in mild astonishment, then slumped against Rick, cackling idiotically into his chest. His body felt firm and supportive, while hers had become completely fluid. She made no attempt to struggle, when, after the slightest hesitation, Rick's arms closed around her. They stayed like that for a moment, neither of them moving and nothing seemed very funny any more. Celia lifted her face. Rick looked down impassively. 'Not tonight, Rick . . . please,' she begged softly.

He released her so abruptly Celia almost fell over. The bones of his jaw seized up with rigid anger and the contemptuous words came squeezed out through clenched teeth like toothpaste from a tube. 'You needn't worry on that count. I usually like my women to be conscious when I'm making love to them.' The cruelty was very neat.

Celia shrank away, flinching as if Rick had struck her across the mouth. 'I'm not drunk,' she lied miserably, and wondered whether all this was really happening or was a distortion of her drink-befuddled brain.

'Drunk enough. You already had too much at the reception.'

She had turned away from him. 'Ahah!' she swung back—too quickly, and felt the room swirl around her. 'So you were counting!' The small spark of triumph made her voice high and childish. 'Lucy said . . .'

'I'm not interested in your sister's inane pronouncements,' Rick cut her off tersely. 'Can you walk or do I have to carry you?'

She felt so wretched nothing mattered any more, not even keeping up a front. 'I don't know,' Celia mumbled.

With an arm around her waist Rick got her into the bedroom and eased her down into a sitting position on the bed. The moment he took away the supporting hand, Celia flopped sideways on to the bed and closed her eyes. It rather felt like being on a ship . . . the gentle swirling motion around her. It would have been soothing if it hadn't been for the accompanying nauseous churning in her stomach. 'Leave me alone,' she mouthed, thinking she was shouting, as Rick's hands pushed her this way and that, peeling off the tunic and dragging it down over her limp frame. Part of her brain was still functioning enough to take in what he was doing. In a moment she would summon up the energy to sit up and stop him.

The blue crêpe dress hung askew on the hanger suspended from the top of the wardrobe door; a clear dash of colour against the subdued pale wood of the wardrobe. It was the first thing Celia's eyes focused on when she unglued her eyelids the next morning.

Rick had done it deliberately, of course—left the dress hanging there so she would see it the moment she opened her eyes and feel humiliated. Celia wrenched her eyes away. A small ray of reason told her she was being irrational. She could have just as easily woken on her other side and not noticed the dress until later. If she felt sick with humiliation she had enough reason on her own count without becoming paranoid about Rick's motives.

To be fair—and that was not easy—she had to admit he had behaved with amazing restraint considering he was landed with a tipsy wife on his wedding night. Tipsy? Drunk, Celia corrected herself without emotion. She had been dead drunk, but certainly had not been a wife. She pulled out her left hand from under the bedclothes and studied the band of white gold with detached interest. Rick should have insisted on exchanging cast-iron contracts, not rings in front of the minister yesterday—and with Mr Burgess on the sidelines to explain legal technicalities to the congregation. Celia gave a dry laugh and pushed the covers back to get up. 'Oh my God,' she groaned and stared in dumbstruck disbelief at the wispy white nightgown—what there was of it, and that wasn't much. Her breasts were climbing out of the microscopic lace bodice and the rest of it was gossamer sheer.

Eleanor had foiled her after all. The 'trousseau' had been one of the many bones of contention during the last week. Celia had gone out and bought a couple of swiss cotton nighties and Eleanor, throwing her hands up in elegant horror, had raced off and come back with a virtual shopful of painfully seductive concoctions. Celia refused point-blank to have them, but hadn't allowed for her mother's deviousness in engineering a swap somewhere along the line. Her suitcase must be full of the rubbish—and Rick would have seen them and thought ... what? That she was planning to trot out some pathetic seduction routine, only had been too drunk to carry it off?

Celia had a vivid picture of Rick manoeuvring her unconscious form into the ghastly garment and flushed hot and cold with mortification. Why couldn't he have left her in her slip if he had to undress her at all?

'You're awake I see,' Rick said, pleasantly, strolling into the room.

Celia yanked the bedclothes up to her chin. Rick was already dressed in jeans and a casual shirt and looked remarkably fit—and surprisingly cheerful. Instantly she was on the alert with suspicion.

Rick settled himself on the edge of the bed. 'I've ordered breakfast. It'll be up in a few minutes if you think you can face it.' Too sympathetic for words. Celia stiffened under the covers. 'Why don't you take a shower before it arrives—you'll feel a lot better.' Rick smiled down into her wary eyes.

She was at a disadvantage almost prone with Rick looking down at her face. Celia drew herself up to a sitting position, still holding the bedclothes under her chin, forgetting that there wasn't much of her that he hadn't seen the previous night. 'I'm fine, thank you!' She managed a tepid smile. She felt much better than she deserved. Instead of nursing a colossal hangover she was barely aware of the slightly uncomfortable sensation behind her forehead. Her eyes drifted to the blue dress.

Rick followed her gaze. 'I hung it up so it wouldn't get crushed,' he explained carelessly.

'Thank you,' Celia murmured, reddening. 'About last night, I . . .'

'Forget it,' Rick muttered gruffly and touched her bare arm—possibly in a gesture of reassurance. She moved it abruptly out of range.

'How can I? I made a fool of myself,' Celia burst out, perversely angry that Rick didn't want to discuss it, while she felt compelled to drag out the sorry incident into the open.

'I said forget it.' Rick's voice rose a fraction and he got up off the bed. He moved to the window and stared out moodily while Celia studied him side-on.

Last night, in his dark suit, he had looked completely at home in the sophisticated setting, but in the morning light he somehow looked wrong—too big and brown amongst the pretentious subtlety.

'Where did you sleep?' Celia asked before she could stop herself.

Rick turned from the window. 'In the other bedroom. I was quite comfortable.'

'Sorry,' she mumbled.

He ignored that. 'We're flying back to Mandarah today.'

'Mandarah? I thought you said . . .'

'The islands can wait—it wasn't such a good idea any more than this was.' He glanced around the large room. 'It stinks. You did want to go straight back, didn't you? Well, didn't you?' Rick persisted sharply when she didn't answer.

Did she? Celia was not sure about that any more. She thought of Addie and Susan and everybody else on the property, as well as the family, finding out that the honeymoon had been a fiasco and had ended before it even began. She didn't think her pride could take such a battering, nor being the object of inevitable curiosity while they went through their first turbulent paces as newly-weds. That was best done out of range of people they both knew, and that meant as far away from Mandarah as possible.

Other thoughts ran through her mind. Mandarah meant no excuses . . . no blotting herself out on champagne in the evenings. The islands, even this hotel in the middle of a bustling city, seemed much less threatening an alternative. Rick was waiting for an answer. 'I don't want to upset your arrangements,' Celia ventured politely, and realised immediately she had said the wrong thing. Rick would think she was sniping about his unilateral arrangements. 'I mean, I'm quite happy to go along with the idea of an island holiday.' She would have choked on the word 'honeymoon'.

Rick's eyes narrowed. 'Are you trying to tell me you want to go on the honeymoon after all?' he asked, with careful restraint.

'Well, I . . . I suppose so.'

'Damn it, Celia, I give up trying to work you out!' The restraint was short-lived. 'One minute you're furious because I was going to keep you away from that wretched place, then the next, you're acting as if it's the last place you want to go.' The angry flush streaked Rick's tanned face unevenly. 'Well, it's too late now. I've just cancelled the bookings for everything and I'm not about to ring them up and rebook. Besides which I really don't want to be away from Mandarah at this particular time . . . the flooding . . .'

'Oh so that's it, is it? I might have known! *You* want to go back, so we're going back—it's got nothing at all to do with me. You couldn't care less how I feel—you never did, so why bother trying to make out that you've changed everything on my account?'

Rick was at the bed in a stride. 'What the hell is it with you, Celia? I'd like to shake you till your teeth rattled.'

Celia shrank back waiting for him to do it; his eyes were angry, but puzzled too. The knock on the door of the suite came in the nick of time. Rick moved to the door. 'You'd better hurry if you want breakfast. I'm not serving it in bed.'

In the doorway he turned, eyes dropping to her hands, still clutching the bedclothes. 'You'll get cramp if you hang on to that for much longer.'

CHAPTER EIGHT

THEY left Sydney mid-afternoon via one of the commercial airlines and picked up Rick's plane at Brisbane airport. They had finished sniping at each other hours ago at the hotel and from then on Celia had retreated behind a wall of sullen silence. When she got bored with flipping through the stack of magazines she had bought for the flight she tried staring out the window. It was just as boring and in the end, she put her head back and closed her eyes.

It was as if someone had pressed the replay button on a video machine; Rick at the controls, the engine buzzing in her ears and the air thick with tension. Every now and then Celia had to sneak a look down at the ring on her finger to confirm that she wasn't in a time warp.

The sound of the engine changed as they dropped height. Home, she thought with an awful sinking feeling that had nothing to do with the descent, and opened her eyes. 'Will Addie be back yet—at Mandarah?' she tried to make the question sound like casual interest and mentally crossed her fingers that Rick would say 'no' and she'd be spared the scrutiny of those shrewd old eyes that would size up the situation in a flash.

Rick cast her a sidelong glance through his dark lashes. 'Worried about what she's thinking about the newly-weds? he asked sardonically.

Piqued that she was so transparent, Celia gave an angry shrug. 'No, she won't be there,' Rick went on tartly, 'she'll be returning with my parents to spend a couple of weeks with them, so you can relax. I especially asked her not to come back for a while.' His voice tightened like his mouth. 'You might be concerned about appearances but I want this marriage to work and I'm going to make damn sure it gets a chance without a helping hand from anyone on the sidelines.'

Celia made an involuntary sound like the start of a harsh laugh. 'I'm sure you will,' she agreed acidly and, aware of Rick's eyes on her, lifted her chin defiantly and looked straight ahead.

'It does take two, in case it's slipped your mind,' Rick muttered, checking his temper, or possibly saving it for when he could let it rip at a more convenient time.

'If you're referring to the terms of our arrangement, I'm sure I won't be given the opportunity to forget them. Don't worry, I intend keeping my end of the deal,' Celia said shakily—and meant it, only wishing she could rid her mind of the picture of the previous night. It made her cringe, but last night was nerves and it wouldn't happen again, she reassured herself. One humiliating episode was enough and she had no intention of repeating the performance. Her eyes fell to the controls where Rick's knuckles stood out tightly, their colour matching the colour of the white gold of his wedding ring. Rick was furious. Good. Celia sat back, satisfied that her reaction had needled him. A moment later she was regretting it.

Rick brought the plane down with an un-accustomed jolt, taxied furiously and pulled up so sharply she was thrown forward, with the seatbelt straining painfully against her waist. 'Rick!' Celia called out in alarm, then shaken, sat silent and fuming while the small plane edged along to a gentle stop. 'What were you trying to do—kill me?' she demanded when she got her breath back from the fright.

Rick swore harshly, then turned to her, white-faced with his own shock. 'Are you all right?' His voice was unsteady and husky with concern. 'I'm sorry, that was a damned crazy thing to do. Are you all right?' he asked again and Celia nodded angrily.

Her legs felt like jelly and she let Rick help her out of the plane but pulled away from him the moment her feet touched ground. Rick reached out, wanting to touch her again and thought better of it. He dropped his hands to his sides. 'Sure you're okay?'

'Quite. No thanks to you,' Celia returned in a huff. 'And if you're planning to do away with me for my share of the property, you'd do better to try something a little less obvious than staging a crash on Mandarah's doorstep,' she sneered into Rick's shocked face.

Leaving him to get the suitcases out, Celia started towards the house. She walked slowly, more shaken than she had let on. When she reached the lawn in front of the main house she stopped and waited for Rick to catch up. If they were going to put up a front it would look better if they gave the impression they were still talking to each other. She composed her face into a bland mask for Susan and any other staff that might happen by.

She need not have bothered. There was no welcoming committee in evidence. The nearby yards were empty and there was no sign of anyone until they stepped into the hall and Susan came down the corridor at a great rate.

'You've arrived then,' she called out the obvious from about five yards away with her customary brusqueness, and no surprise. Not a skerrick of surprise showed on the wrinkled features from close range either. 'You'll be wanting your dinner when you've changed. It's all cold, so I'll set it up in the dining room and you can help yourselves when you're ready. You'll probably want an early night.' She looked Celia full in the face for the first time. 'You're very pale and could do with a lie down by the look of you—the room's prepared.'

'Yes. Thank you, Susan,' Rick replied—courteously, but no one could mistake the dismissal in his voice, not even Susan, who could be very obtuse when she chose. The grim look on Rick's face must have decided her not to loiter. 'Well, if there's nothing else . . .'

Celia gave the housekeeper a quick smile. 'I . . . we are rather tired . . . it's been a long flight.'

One hurdle over, Celia thought relieved as Susan disappeared in the direction of the kitchen, then was irritated with herself for her childishness. Who cared what interpretation Susan put on their premature return? She was hardly going to demand an explanation for the truncated honeymoon—nor was anyone else for that matter.

Celia started down the corridor, Rick a step behind her. Passing the door of her old room, she suddenly stopped, then very deliberately, reached out and placed her hand on the doorknob.

In an instant Rick had the suitcase on the floor and his fingers over her hand. 'Just where do you think you're going?'

All she wanted was some time to herself—some breathing space out of range of Rick's precarious temper. It had been worth a try. 'I forgot,' she lied coldly, resisting the fleeting temptation to plead with him.

'Like hell you did.' Rick peeled her fingers away from the knob. 'You know where our room is,' he said curtly, going on ahead, and after a moment's hesitation, Celia followed—like a dutiful wife. She might as well start getting used to the role.

The room was the largest bedroom in the house and used to be her mother and father's— and her grandfather and grandmother's years before that. It was a lovely room with lots of mellowed wood and old lace drapes over the french windows that led out on to the verandah. The enormous bed, with its ornately carved bedhead, had been brought to the homestead by Sam's parents late last century and was solid enough to see out another hundred years. It drew her eyes like a magnet and the more Celia tried not to look at it, the more her eyes kept straying to it. She caught Rick's eyes—watching her too carefully.

He put the case down on the floor. 'I'll get the other things out of the plane later. You should have let me collect the remainder of your stuff from George's before we left Sydney—we could have brought it back with us.'

And broadcast everything to a host of avidly curious relatives? No thank you, she would rather have gone about naked. 'I've got enough in the case, thank you,' Celia said icily, 'and Eleanor will be sending the rest on in a week or two—she didn't think they'd be needed quite so soon—and she wasn't the only one,' Celia added with heavy sarcasm in case Rick had forgotten she was still mad at him for the last minute change of plans.

Rick ignored the jibe. 'I'll see you shortly.'

Celia raced through a shower at breakneck speed, not trusting Rick to be away for more than a few minutes. The green sunfrock clung damply to her back where she had missed with the towel in her hurry. She must have set some sort of record getting to the lounge but was there, prowling around like a restless cat, for almost half an hour before she heard Rick come back into the house.

He was carrying a tray when he came into the room. 'I thought we'd eat in here, if you don't mind eating off your knee. That dining room always seems to need a dozen people in it to take the edge off its resemblance to a baronial dining hall.' Rick gave a tentative smile that looked as if was testing out the muscles around his mouth. 'Sit down, I'll bring it over.'

Celia left her position by the window and strolled casually to the sofa. 'Thank you,' she

murmured with an excess of politeness as she
seated herself on the edge of the sofa. Then she
noticed the uncorked bottle of champagne and the
two glasses, already filled. She looked sharply at
Rick in surprise that quickly turned into
suspicion. Champagne? After last night? What
was Rick playing at? 'I don't think I'm up to
more champagne,' she said coldly.

'I'm sure you can manage one glass,' Rick
replied with a smile and didn't sound as if he was
mocking.

Celia shrugged ungraciously and took the glass
while a flock of butterflies suddenly went
fluttering in all directions inside her stomach.
She wasn't so thick that she couldn't guess what
Rick was playing at—declaring a timely truce for
a very obvious purpose.

She ate because she was hungry but five
minutes later could not have said whether she'd
eaten chicken or cheese. She took two sips of the
champagne and left the rest, toying nervously
with the stem of the glass while Rick kept up a
flow of one-sided conversation. It was impossible
to concentrate on what he was saying when her
mind kept projecting to that enormous bed, and
her nerves were in shreds waiting for the dreadful
moment when he would stop talking and suggest
. . . suggest? who was she kidding? that they turn
in for the night.

Rick's words washed over her in an indistinguishable stream, almost soothingly. Celia
began to relax—if unfreezing from rigidity to
mere stiffness was a measure of relaxation. Rick
was talking to her as if she was a wild filly he was

trying to break in. The analogy struck her as ironically appropriate. Celia suddenly gave an involuntary smile.

Rick moved closer to her on the sofa. 'What are you smiling about?'

'Me . . . you . . . us,' she said glibly.

Rick's face darkened. 'And just what do you find so amusing about us?' There was an edge in his voice that should have warned her to watch her step. 'The way you're talking to me . . . just as if I were a horse you're about to break in—it struck me as rather apt.'

'That's a cynical way of putting it.'

'It's true though, isn't it? You were just talking to . . . well, you were just talking.'

'Talking to soften you up?' Rick suggested mockingly while his eyes sparked angrily. 'I suppose it wouldn't occur to you that I might have been talking about Mandarah and other things because I thought you'd be interested?' he said, bitterly.

'Of course I'm interested,' Celia protested with a sudden flush of guilt.

Rick smiled mirthlessly. 'Then what was I saying just now?'

She tried to think. 'Something about rivers . . . the river—oh, I don't know,' she snapped, exasperated. 'You should have warned me that I'd be cross-examined on every word that dropped from your lips.' Slamming her glass down on the coffee table, Celia got off the sofa and moved huffily to the window. 'I don't remember it being in your terms. You should have put them in writing.'

'Must you always refer to our marriage that way? Damn it, it's more than just a set of terms.' Rick reacted with harsh anger.

'Not with me it isn't!' Celia threw back at him. 'And I don't know why you bother with the pretence, when we both know our so-called marriage is a sham. You pushed me into it to get your hands on the property—I'm not blaming you,' she got in hastily, not liking the expression of Rick's face. 'I wanted my share too, that's why I let myself be railroaded into it. I didn't exactly have much choice though, did I?' she finished on a peevish note.

Rick rasped out a short grating laugh. 'You're a great one for kidding yourself, aren't you? You agreed willingly enough, so don't start implying that I kidnapped you and dragged you protesting to the altar. If you wanted out, you had almost two weeks to pull out. Why didn't you?'

'Don't imagine I didn't think about it after you bundled me off to Sydney!'

'Then you had the ideal opportunity, so why didn't you take it?' Rick asked, with a hint of a cynical smile lurking around the corners of his mouth.

Full of resentment at being put on the spot, Celia looked at him while the reasons floated through her mind. She couldn't face the thought of Mandarah being sold up ... or Addie being left without a home. They went without saying, yet at bottom it was probably that she felt too numb to resist, once Eleanor had set the wedding juggernaut into motion. It didn't sound much of a reason. Celia shrugged for an answer.

Rick's eyes combed her face very carefully. 'You wanted to marry, Celia,' he said dispassionately and watched her face blanch. 'Otherwise, Mandarah or no Mandarah, wild horses would not have dragged you to the altar. You can't admit that to me because you can't even admit it to yourself.'

She wanted to laugh, and couldn't. 'Don't be absurd,' she said, shocked, then rallied angrily and unthinkingly moved towards him. 'Of all the conceit! I suppose you think you're such a prize no female could possibly not want to marry you. Well, get this clear, Rick Harland, I may have imagined I wanted to marry you once, but not this time. You're just a means to an end and if you think differently, then you're out of your mind.' She stood, arms akimbo, glaring down at him searching for words to wipe that cynical twist off his face. They came in a wild moment of inspiration. 'I haven't exactly been pining for you these last four years, as you surely must have noticed when you came spying on me in London,' Celia sneered, and experienced a stab of smug triumph as Rick's smile contorted into a grimace. Point to her. In the middle of her self-congratulatory smirk Rick flung himself off the sofa and grasped her arm savagely.

'You were thinking about him last night, weren't you?' he hissed at her with his face so close the pores of his skin appeared all dots—like a newspaper photograph.

Off-guard, Celia was slow to react. 'Who?'

The mechanical question seemed to incense

him. 'Don't play the innocent with me.' Rick
shook her like a rag doll.

And then Celia understood—and laughed, right
into his face, partly from repressed fright and
partly from the utter absurdity of Rick's innuendo.
The situation was whirling out of control and she
with it on the wave of hysterical laughter.

Rick raised his hand. He's going to slap me,
Celia thought fleetingly and came to her senses.
Her mouth clamped shut like a trapdoor, the
sudden fit over. Rick didn't slap her. He gripped
her arms again and he hurt her. 'Ouch, let me
go!' She tried to twist herself out of his hold and
that only made it hurt more. Eyes smarting, Celia
gave up in frustration. 'God, that must make you
feel powerful!'

'You were thinking about him last night,
weren't you? Wishing it was him instead of me
who wanted to make love to you—that's why you
had to drink yourself into oblivion.'

She stared in a distant fascination at the
stranger she had known all her life, and to whom,
God help her, she was married. She opened her
mouth to tell him he was crazy. 'Dear me, jealous
are we?' The unpremeditated jeer came out
instead. She was fuelling the insane situation and
she knew it, but was past caring. The need to
hurt back was too overpowering.

Rick's fingers dug their way deeper into her
arms almost pushing through the flesh to the
bone. 'Jealous? Me, jealous? Of that androgynous
little twerp?' The strangled snarl stuck halfway
down his throat. 'I wonder that he can
manage . . .'

'Don't you dare insult Kel like that!' Celia rose to her friend's defence with more fierceness than she would have used to defend herself. Kel was not especially masculine-looking, but Rick's innuendo was way off mark. 'Just because he's not a macho gorilla like some people, doesn't mean he's what you think.'

'So you were thinking about him!' Rick shouted in a frenzied triumph as if the mention of Kel's name was a confirmation of his wild accusation. 'I knew it!' He grinned crazily at her and Celia felt a twist of real alarm. She glowered back but stayed silent. Incensed she might be, but she was not an idiot. One more push and the last shred of Rick's self-control would be gone, and Celia didn't think much of her chances if that happened. Rick had murder in his eyes.

After a long moment in which they could have committed every fleck in each other's irises to heart, Celia said, very quietly, 'I think you might let go of my arms now.'

Rick came out of the long stare shaken. He unclamped his hands and let them fall to his sides. With the gesture, a blank mask slipped over the distorted whiteness of his features. He expelled his breath in a shuddering sigh and turned away from her.

Celia wanted to run, but made herself walk out of the room calmly, not even slamming the door behind her. There was no point in running; her feet were too unsteady and there was nowhere to run anyway. She was not in the city now, where at eight-thirty in the evening the streets bustled with people and noise, and there were any number of restaurants and cinemas to disappear into. This was Mandarah—hundreds and hundreds of miles around her and nowhere to hide.

She met Susan along the corridor. 'Finished dinner? Good. You get a good night's rest now.' The housekeeper nodded approvingly in the mistaken assumption that Celia was on her way to the bedroom.

As Susan bustled away Celia turned her steps towards the bedroom. Why not? Rick would find her anywhere in the house when he was ready and she was past putting up any sort of resistance. And she wasn't frightened of him either, Celia told herself, trying to blot out the vision of the murderous grey eyes.

In the bedroom she drew aside the heavy curtains and stood at the window taking deep breaths to ease the dry tightness inside her lungs. The last of the twilight was melting into darkness over the hills in the distance, casting its final translucent streaks of colour across the sky that very soon would turn into the navy-black that she loved so much. Last night she had wanted the comfort of the familiar canopy, Celia remembered with a sour taste in her mouth. Well, she had it now—the precious sky, the vast empty spaces full of silence—and for good measure, Rick Harland. What more could a girl wish for, she asked herself bitterly. And she had got them all just by trading in her self-respect.

She had not been alone in that, but it was small consolation that Rick was feeling every bit as self-disgusted. He had to be or he wouldn't be trying so hard to kid himself they had any chance of making a go of their sham marriage. Nor would he be consoling his battered pride with the fantasy that she had married him for love and not a half share in Mandarah. In a curious way, Rick seemed to find it more difficult than she did, to accept the reality of their situation, going off half-cocked into fits of temper and insane jealousy.

That was his problem and she was not going to go out of her way to make it easier for him, Celia thought angrily. They had both paid too high a price for their dream—or was it their greed? Either way, each of them would have to make the best of it. They had made a deal and if Rick was expecting her to renege on it, he was in for a surprise. She was going to be ready for him.

'Damn Mandarah,' Celia cursed softly, turning away from the rapidly gathering darkness. In the half light the enormous bed formed a menacing mound in the far end of the room. Celia stared at it impassively. Whoever had made up the proverb about making your bed and lying on it certainly had known what they were talking about.

With sudden decision she crossed the room and switching on the bedside lamp, drew back the covers of the bed with deliberate care. Her mind felt as if it had just emerged through a wringer—flat and utterly emotionless. When she finished with the bed, Celia moved to her suitcase. Kneeling beside it she riffled through the 'trousseau' collection, compliments of Eleanor, and selected a nightgown at random. It was indistinguishable from the one Rick had crammed her into last night, and may have even been the same one. Celia couldn't tell and didn't care.

Undressing completely, she put it on quickly in case she changed her mind, and was at the wardrobe putting away her dress when Rick walked in. Her heart landed in her mouth in one jump and her hand jerked the hangers, sending them swinging against each other. 'I'm ready for bed when you are,' Celia said in the most off-hand voice she was able to produce and went on with what she was doing—or would have, if her hands hadn't been shaking so much. She heard the intake of Rick's breath across the room.

He closed the distance between them with unhurried agility, like a neatly lithe cat, yet when he stood in front of her Celia saw that his chest was rising and falling in unnaturally rapid rhythm as if he had run a very long way. She didn't move as Rick reached out a hand and very deliberately stroked his fingers up and down her bare arm, watching her face for reaction. She shivered a little but stared impassively into the dark grey pools of wary doubt.

'And what trick have you got up your sleeve now?' The distrust in Rick's voice matched his eyes.

'In case you haven't noticed, I'm not wearing sleeves,' Celia tried to quip, the scratchy voice a dead giveaway.

His eyes left her face and travelling downwards, fastened on her breasts. The scant bit of lacy fabric did not leave anything to the imagination. Rick brought his eyes back to her face. The doubt was still in them but it was giving way to a darkly glittering desire.

'If this is a set-up for a tease, you're going to be very sorry,' Rick warned softly with a velvety smile that was possibly the most threatening thing Celia had seen. She shook her head. There was no way back now and she didn't need Rick's threat to press the point home. The look in his eyes did that.

Just as deliberately as he had stroked her arm, Rick slid his hand around her waist and moving it down over the curve of her hip, pulled her against himself, while his other hand lifted her chin. Their eyes still locked, he slowly brought his mouth down, parting her unresisting lips with a measured pressure.

It was all done with such precision and restraint he might have been demonstrating the first steps of seduction to a class of trainee Casanovas. It left her cold and that did not go unnoticed for long.

Rick pulled back, eyes blazing. 'The ice maiden, so that's your little game, is it? We'll see about that.'

He swept her up in his arms, carried her to the bed and practically dropped her on to it. Leaving her there, Rick began pulling off his clothes, letting them fall in haphazard heaps on to the floor. Unable to help herself, Celia watched in a state of mesmerised shock as he stripped himself down to his briefs without taking his eyes off her. At the last moment, when he was stepping out of his underpants, Celia turned away. Rick laughed softly.

She had expected him to throw himself on her in fury and was seized up with anticipatory fright. But Rick was quite gentle as he lowered her head carefully down on to the pillow. Wide-eyed, Celia stared up at him as propped up on an elbow, Rick positioned himself against her, pinning her down with his body. His mouth was disarmingly restrained as it descended on her lips; his tongue flicked teasingly at the corners of her mouth as his hand eased the strap of her nightgown down over her shoulder and insinuated itself in between the fabric and her flesh. Celia caught back a gasp in her throat.

Rick pulled his mouth away to look at her exposed breast, watching his own hand moving sensuously over the soft roundness, then looking back at her, his heavy-lidded gaze holding her eyes fast as her nipples hardened under his touch. Her lips parted to let her breath out in short shallow gasps that fell into rhythm with Rick's own ragged pattern. He was moving languidly against her thigh and the tantalising contact of hard muscled body through the sheer material set off a chain reaction inside her that started as a series of uncontrollable tremors and heightened into waves of mounting excitement. And all the time Rick watched her face.

Celia felt vulnerable and exposed—and totally helpless as her body stirred and arched volupt-uously under Rick's hand, moving to some primitive beat. Her mind was floating away somewhere out of reach, abandoning her to the flood of sensation. She moaned softly as Rick's mouth settled between her breasts.

Without realizing it, she was cradling his head, holding him to her, her fingers entwining through the thick curls, then kneading hard into his shoulders as the flares inside her sharpened and made her call out in surprised little cries of pleasure.

The nightgown was being eased further and further down her body, Rick's mouth following in its wake. She was babbling incoherently by the time he slid the nightgown over her feet and tossed it to the floor. Celia shivered, then lay still and suddenly silent as Rick knelt on the bed and looked at her. She watched him in a breathless excitement that made the blood pound furiously in her ears as his eyes travelled deliberately slowly down the creamy whiteness of her body. She waited and began to tremble and then couldn't wait any more. 'Rick,' she whispered urgently, raising herself off the pillow and curving a hand around the back of his head, pulling him down with her as she fell back, her mouth parted in eagerness.

In the soft light of the shaded lamp, Rick's eyes glowed into hers, the grey smouldering black like coals. 'Tell me now—that's it me you want. I want to hear you say it,' he breathed raggedly at her.

Her hand went limp at the back of his head as Celia stared at him, wonderingly, the disbelief taking its time to filter through. Kel? Was he harking back to Kel? Now? Celia let her hand fall away from his neck and turned her face away, feeling every bit of warmth draining out of her and a coldness edging in like splinters of ice where the blood had rushed heatedly moments before.

'It's me, Celia—me you want,' Rick rasped, his mouth hot and excited on her ear . . . down her throat.

She stared bleakly at the wall, feeling as if turned into a lump of ice, and sick with the realisation that Rick had been merely seducing her to score a point over her supposed lover . . . and that she had wanted so much to be seduced.

Rick's mouth stilled on her throat. He jerked his head up. 'What is it?' When she didn't answer he grasped her chin and turned her face towards him. 'Don't close up on me like that, for God's sake, Celia.' It was a plea, throbbing with frustration and anger.

Rick rammed his mouth down on her lips, probing savagely for a response that she wouldn't—couldn't give. Not now. The body which he had so expertly manipulated into response was still there for him—it was all he was entitled to.

'What the hell are you thinking of?' Rick's voice shook violently.

'"What"? Don't you mean "Who"?' she shot back with soft viciousness.

In the elongated moment of silence their hearts thumped against each other. 'You bitch!' Rick exploded in a rush of breath. 'You little bitch!' and with all restraint gone, brought his weight down on her and parted her legs roughly.

She didn't fight him until the unexpected stab of pain when he entered her. Celia cried out in shock, she had no idea what, and pushed against him wildly, then fell back against the pillow as Rick took her in a mêlée of rage and desire. He called out her name in a distorted groan and then was very still. When her mind came out of its self-protective blankness, Rick was beside her.

Celia lay in seething silence as Rick touched her shoulder with tentative gentleness. She froze into rigidity but let his hand stay where it was. 'You little idiot, you deliberately let me think . . .'

'That's right, blame me for your paranoia!' she blazed at him in fury.

'Why the hell didn't you tell me?' Rick snarled back, matching her anger with his own. 'I didn't mean to hurt you.'

She looked at him in dislike. 'You didn't,' she said icily, and started to turn away.

Rick caught her face under the chin with one hand. 'You little fool,' he said gruffly in a mixture of tenderness, frustration, and the remnants of his anger. 'I love you.'

In a single movement, Celia pushed his hand away and sprang up into a sitting position. 'Don't say that!' she yelled, something giving way inside her and gushing out in hysteria. 'Don't you ever say that to me again! You got what you were entitled to, leave it there.'

CHAPTER NINE

RICK looked dumbfounded, shock stripping the tan off his face to an ugly ashen. Then the colour came back in slow dark streaks. 'Hell!' he muttered, shutting his eyes and pressing the palm of his hand tightly over the closed lids. He dropped his hand in what was almost a gesture of defeat and stared at her, shaking his head.

Celia waited for him to leave the bed, hating his nearness, oppressively conscious of his nakedness—and hating that too. She was unprepared when Rick grabbed her shoulder and catching her off-guard, pushed her back down onto the pillow. 'I said I love you...can't you understand...?' he rasped harshly into her face.

'Don't say that!' Celia came out of her freeze and struck as hard as she could into his chest with a closed fist. 'I told you not to say that!' She kept on hitting until finally she did not want to hit any more. She must have hurt him but Rick gave no sign of it. 'Let me go,' she said wearily, awash with misery. With the fight drained out of her, Celia closed her eyes to block out the sight of Rick's face that was controlled into an awful grimace. He took his hand away. Celia didn't move; she felt as limp as a rag doll.

'Damn Sam.' She heard Rick mutter in a soft despair.

Her eyes flicked open. 'Oh he's in for it too now, is he?'

Rich clicked his tongue in frustration, then he said abruptly, 'You're tired. We'll talk tomorrow. Why don't you get some sleep now.' His voice softened, 'I'm sorry if I hurt you.'

She believed that but it was his lie that hurt more than his act of possession, and it wasn't the lie he was apologising for. 'You didn't. I've already told you that.' She turned her back on him, not caring whether he stayed or went. Rick was not going to touch her again that night.

Celia woke when someone touched her arm and came out of the deep sleep in a disorientated haze. 'Rick? she murmured sleepily.

'Your tea, Mrs Harland.' The cook's young daughter Jean, smiled into Celia's startled eyes as she placed the tray down on the bedside table. 'Mr Harland left with the men hours ago.'

Instantly Celia sat up. 'Left?'

Jean dropped her eyes quickly and in a flurry of embarrassment, Celia realised she was completely naked and grabbed the covers. 'Left? Oh, yes, I see,' she said flatly, as if Rick's disappearance at dawn was no surprise to her. She gave the girl a smile. 'Thank you, Jean.'

Jean was already at the door. 'It's raining,' she murmured for something to say, her face still pink with embarrassment, and not risking another look at the bed.

Celia frowned after her. So Rick had shot off— for the day most likely if he had gone off with the stockmen. Well, she hadn't wanted to see him any more than he wanted to see her, and she certainly did not want to talk to him. The less they had to do with each other the more pleased she would be. So why the hell was she feeling so miffed? What was the matter with her? Had she expected Rick to hover around all day abjectly apologising for taking her so savagely last night? That would be a laugh. He had said all he was going to say on that matter last night—mouthed those hollow words 'I love you' after throwing the blame on her for letting him believe she'd had previous lovers.

And she had meant him to believe that. The question was: why? Celia picked up the cup and stared out at the drizzle that looked as if it was trying to make up its mind whether to peter out or work itself into a fullscale downpour. She sipped the tea slowly, wondering why she had fanned Rick's jealousy by encouraging the myth that she and Kel had been lovers.

Face-saving? If Rick had realised she was still a virgin his ego would have made him jump to the conclusion that she had been waiting for him— and he would not have been more wrong. But it was a silly face-saver none the less. Rick was bound to find out that she had never slept with a man before; it was not something that was likely to pass unnoticed by a sexually experienced man—and Rick Harland was that all right. He'd had her purring like a cat until that moment when his insane jealousy tripped him up.

Neither aspect was very pleasant to remember, nor was the rest of the ghastly night. Celia rammed the cup down on the saucer and flung herself out of bed. The clothes that had been scattered around the floor the previous night, lay neatly over the back of the chair. How tactful, Celia thought drily.

The bath was a mistake. Soaking in the warm, fragrant water in the deep old-fashioned tub, might be doing wonderful things for her aching body but not a thing for her frazzled mind. The sight of her long, slim body kept triggering off images and sensations she would rather not remember. After several abortive attempts to blot them out, Celia gave up, pulled out the plug and finished off in the shower cubicle. Then dressed in a cotton shirt and skirt, made her way to the kitchen, brightening her expression as she came through the door.

'Good morning Susan,' she sang out with overdone cheerfullness to Susan's scrawny back. 'I'm afraid I slept in ... I was so tired. I'm starving now ... where's cook?' she asked, looking about the kitchen.

Susan turned slowly and came towards her. To Celia's astonishment, Susan took her by the arm and very kindly, as if Celia was an invalid on her first day out of bed, led her to the table. 'Now you just sit yourself down here child. Cook is preparing lunch for the men in the dining hall. I'll see to your breakfast,' she said, voice gruff with kindness. It was not Susan's way to pander to anybody, except perhaps her old friend, Addie. Celia stared, open-mouthed. 'You're not to worry,' the old lady smiled encouragingly. 'He'll be all right—they all will. They've been through that sort of thing before, haven't they?'

'Through what before? What are you talking about? I'm not worried—why should I be?'

It was Susan's turn to stare. In a moment her face readjusted to its regular closed-up look. 'So you haven't heard ... and here I was thinking you were trying to put on a cheerful face ...'

That part was true, but obviously not for the reason Susan thought. 'For heaven's sake, Susan, stop talking in riddles and tell me what's going on.'

'I though Jean would have told you ...'

'She told me that ... my husband ...' Celia tested the word out and didn't like it. 'She told me Rick went off a couple of hours ago with the men—what's so unusual about that?' Her voice sharpened as Susan returned to the stove. 'Just where have they gone?'

Susan removed the pan of eggs from the hotplate and slowly began to dish them onto a plate. Celia could have shaken her.

'Bill Harrison from Keldon Downs radioed in around dawn ...' Susan started and Celia knew.

'The river! Oh no!' Her hand flew to her mouth in horror. 'It's broken its banks and ...' She couldn't go on as the awful vision rose before her.

'Not yet, and pray God, they'll have got the levees up in time ... if they haven't, then the Harrisons' homestead is a goner,' Susan muttered lugubriously. 'Harrison asked for as many men as we could spare. Rick and the best part of a dozen men took off in two vehicles immediately.'

'Why didn't he tell me?' Celia's voice rose on a wail.

'Didn't want to disturb you,' Susan returned tartly, placing the plate abruptly on the table, voice and action both making plain that she thought Rick's concern misguided—and Celia could only agree.

'He should have told me. Did he leave any message?' she asked in a vague, inexplicable hope.

'Only to say that we should be ready to put up some of the Harrison folk if need be. I can attend to that ... I've done it before,' Susan muttered unsympathetically.

Her appetite had vanished completely. Celia pushed the untouched plate aside. 'I didn't realise the flooding was so close ... we flew over some pretty bad areas on the way back yesterday, but I just didn't think it was as close as Keldon.'

'Doesn't take much this time of year—you should remember that. One downpour in the wrong place can do a lot of damage, and the Harrisons' place has always been a prime target, what with sitting right on top of that stretch of river and no high ground for miles.' Susan sounded as if she was blaming the hapless Harrisons for their ancestors' choice of location. Celia read the concern behind the old lady's belligerence.

They were all only too familiar with the havoc wreaked to stock and property—and sometimes human life, by floods. 'I'll help you get things ready ... in case they get evacuated,' Celia volunteered, miserable with guilt.

Rick had tried to tell her yesterday evening. He must have been worried then and wanted to talk about it. And she hadn't paid the slightest attention to what he had been saying because she had assumed he was only trying to soften her up to get her into bed as soon as he could. At the hotel in Sydney too, Rick had mentioned his concern about the floods, insisting they return home, and she had flared up like a rocket at him for the change of plans because they hadn't suited her. How selfish could one get? she railed at herself, gutted by self-contempt.

All morning Celia worked with Susan and Jean. They went through the linen room checking the bedding, and then prepared the spare bedrooms. After that, Susan sent her into the larder to check the supplies there, although it was a standing joke in the homestead that the old housekeeper knew to a tin, exactly what provisions were in stock at any given moment. Celia did as she was told. It was not until about midway through the afternoon that it dawned on her that Susan was going out of her way to keep her occupied. That was when the alarm really set in. 'There's no real danger, is there? I mean to the men . . .?' she pleaded for reassurance, and while she said 'men' Celia meant Rick.

'They know how to look after themselves. Most of them have been through it before,' was all that Susan would commit herself to saying and it was not the reassurance Celia needed, although what she expected the old lady to come up with, she didn't know herself.

No one turned up that day. There was a strange sense of expectancy . . . of quiet desolation about the place. The yards were ominously silent. Most of the men who hadn't gone with Rick were out somewhere on the property moving stock on to higher ground as a precautionary measure. The heat was oppressive and the drizzle had worked itself into a steady rain that meant to stay. Riding was out, even if she could have brought herself to leave the house, and there was nothing to do except wait.

By evening Celia was seized up with anxiety. White-faced and aching with tiredness, she hung about Susan like a child afraid to be left alone for a minute.

'You'd best go to bed. There's no point in waiting up,' Susan said matter-of-factly, then with all the wrinkles of her face softening visibly, she patted Celia's shoulder awkwardly. 'There's no need to worry child, he'll be all right.'

Celia spent a ghastly night, jerking up at the slightest sound and in the morning felt like death. The house was ready for any emergency; they had stacks of extra blankets piled up, campbeds dragged out of storage cupboards, first aid kits at the ready—and no one came. There was no word from Rick either, and the half-hope that he might send some message, flickered out. A man desperately stacking sandbags against rising water would have other things on his mind than radioing messages to someone who hadn't shown a shred of concern for anyone but herself, Celia reminded herself pointedly.

She sat about listlessly for most of the day until Susan brought out all of Mandarah's silver and virtually ordered her to clean it. It took hours, but not long enough, and when she had finished, Celia was tempted to redo it all over again. She couldn't eat, and refused dinner just as she had refused lunch. At the end of the long day, Susan frogmarched her off to the bedroom muttering things about having enough on her hands without adding a prospective invalid to the list.

Celia undressed down to her slip and wrapping Rick's towelling robe around herself for comfort, prepared to wait out the night. She lay on the bed, listening for sounds until the effort almost made her ears ache, and sprang into alertness at every creak of the floorboards, subsiding wearily as each time the sounds died into stillness. In spite of herself, she did drift into an uneasy sleep, then woke startled, instantly alert, and convinced she had definitely heard something at last.

Barefooted, Celia hurtled out of the room and into Susan's arms. The housekeeper's usually tidy knot of grey hair jutted out in a clump from her head and her skinny form was wrapped in a robe that had been flung on inside out.

'Where is he?' Celia gripped the old lady's arm so fiercely that Susan winced with pain.

'In the Manager's flat. I was coming to fetch you.'

Celia sprinted along the main corridor, then the back passage, through the side door and across the yard. The door to the master bedroom of the flat was open, the light on. She stood at the door and stared.

Rick lay stretched full-length on his back on the bed, mudstained, unshaven, his clothes sticking damply all the way from the clay-caked boots up. 'Oh my God!' Celia sprang to the bed.

'Leave him be, love, he's exhausted,' Susan panted in an unnecessary whisper from the doorway; Rick looked as if a bomb under the bed would not wake him. 'I don't think he's slept since he left here yesterday morning.' Susan came closer to the bed and gazed down at her bedraggled employer, her face wrinkling over with compassion.

Celia wasn't listening. 'Help me with the boots, Susan,' she ordered.

They got the boots off, and by manoeuvring the dead weight of the body around like a bag of cement, managed to remove the sodden clothes as well. Throughout all their efforts, Rick lay dead to the world. When they had stripped him down to his underpants, Susan headed to the door. 'I'll leave you now ... there's the other men to see to ...'

Celia hardly noticed she was gone. She stood by the bed looking down at the inert, exhausted body then drew up the sheet and tucked it around Rick's shoulders. Unthinkingly, she touched his cheek, stroking her hand gently over the stubble. 'Oh, Rick,' she whispered, so relieved she wanted to cry.

As she took the hand away Rick's eyelids flickered but his eyes stayed shut. 'Stay with me, Celia,' he murmured. 'Please ...' and without a word Celia pulled back the sheet and climbed into the bed.

Positioning herself so that she was able to cradle his head with her arm, she drew up the sheet over both of them. Rick nestled in against her, murmuring something indistinct. 'Go back to sleep,' she ordered softly and felt his body relax as he gave a deep, drawn-out sigh. In a couple of seconds the regular rate of his breathing told her he was alseep, and carefully, so as not to disturb him, Celia reached over him to the lamp and put out the light.

After a few moments of pitch black, the darkness thinned out into shadowy greys and she could make out Rick's face lying against her breast, vulnerable and trusting as he abandoned himself to her in sleep. As she watched him something welled up inside her with a physical pain. She fought it with blind instinct. 'I can't ... not again. I can't love this man again,' she mouthed in voiceless protest as the shocking truth struck home.

It had been there all the time—tightly repressed in her mind and just waiting for a moment to spring itself on her—the realisation that she had never stopped loving Rick ... never stopped wanting him. Whatever she had told herself so desperately, it was not Mandarah she wanted. It had not been Mandarah that had set off the chords of homesickness and dissatisfaction, making her ache to come home all those months ago. Mandarah did not matter a hoot without Rick; the last two days of sheer annihilating misery and fear had shown her that.

'Oh God,' Celia cried aloud and Rick stirred uneasily. She buried her face in the dark curls. 'Shh, it's all right,' she whispered, and gathered him closer, wanting the feel of his heavy warmth against her. 'It's all right,' she soothed him, hurting like mad because she knew it could never be all right.

She had come full circle—loving a man who did not love her—the same man, only it did not feel the same as when she had been seventeen.

This time her love took in caring and needing, and being afraid for him—a grown-up love. And it would be a grown-up loneliness she would feel when she left this time.

Left? Instinct had shot ahead of her thoughts and when her mind caught up with it Celia felt shattered. She had to leave. It was as obvious as it was cowardly, but it was self-preservation because in the long term, running away would be easier to bear than years, or a lifetime, with a man who had married her for Mandarah and not for love.

She didn't blame him for that. She had done the same thing herself—or thought she had. The malicious irony was that she could have stayed if her motives had remained repressed, but not now. It would hurt too much to see Rick every day, to love him ... want him, without being loved in return.

So what if he mouthed the words during lovemaking as he had done last night. Even without experience Celia imagined most men would be gallant enough to pay lip-service to that particular little ritual—after all, wasn't that what a woman expected to hear? It was no more than a thank you for the favour, and if Rick ever said it to her again she would probably leap out of the bed, jump into a vehicle and drive off without coming back.

She did not want that to happen. No, Celia resolved she would leave with dignity—as soon as she worked out how. It might take weeks but in the end she would leave. She watched the dawn breaking in streaky fingers of light over the far-off paddocks and felt cold and exhausted. Taking her arm away from around Rick's head she slid down into the bed and closed her eyes. She surfaced from the dreamless sleep and opening her eyes found herself staring into Rick's face, inches above her own. Their positions reversed, he was propped up on an elbow, his expression unreadable. They stayed like that for an infinite moment, neither moving, then impulsively Celia stretched out a hand to his cheek and ran her finger over the stubble, following it down Rick's cheek and along the jawline.

Their eyes stayed locked as the hand continued its downward path, tracing a line down his throat and into the dark curling hair on his chest. Rick's breathing quickened while her own seemed to have stopped altogether as her hand roamed caressingly.

Celia suddenly stopped and reaching both hands around the back of his head drew his face down slowly.

It was a long kiss, sweet and unhurried, sending a slow flow of warmth meandering through her. Without interrupting the kiss, Rick pulled her robe open, slipped his hand around her and held her tightly. Celia melted against him, and with no barrier in her mind, let herself drift along the wave of desire, undulating with languid sensuousness against the length of his body as she gently urged on his desire with her own.

The kiss ended, too soon, when Rick took his mouth away. Eyes bright, breathing out of beat, he touched her cheek gently. 'I'm rubbing your skin raw. Not now ... not with me like this. I have to go back to the Harrisons' in an hour or so, but I'll be back this evening ... I promise.' His mouth curved smilingly and his eyes promised her the world.

The warmth ebbing out of her, Celia stared in dismay. How could she tell him that it would be too late then—that she wanted him now—before the barriers rose up in her mind again ... before she allowed herself to care that he didn't love her? She gave a slight nod and Rick climbed out of the bed, totally unselfconscious.

Celia looked away from him. 'I'll bring back a robe,' she said off-handedly, getting out of the bed herself.

Rick was in the bathroom when she returned, singing out inane ditties with off-key exuberance. He sounded as happy as the proverbial sandboy and she felt wretched. Throwing the robe on to the bed Celia went back into the house to dress, then joined him in the breakfast room.

Having taken it upon herself to attend to their breakfast, Susan pottered in and out, keeping up a disjointed commentary on floods she had known. Celia derived a vague sense of safety from the housekeeper's presence, and was only too aware that it was because she was afraid of being left alone with Rick in case she betrayed either her love or that she was planning to leave him.

She managed to keep up a flow of questions about the Harrisons ... the river, and anything impersonal that came into her head, and considering the turmoil in there already, thought she was making a pretty good job of it when Rick looked up from his plate. 'What's up?' he asked with no particular expression.

Caught in the mental act of throwing bouquets at herself, Celia started. 'What do you mean? That I'm a bit down? I'm tired I guess . . .' she shrugged. 'I was worried about you . . . it's just a reaction, the tiredness . . . I haven't slept much,' she overexplained in her nervousness

Rick let it be, but Celia was not sure she had convinced him. 'I'll feel better later,' she offered, wishing she could leave the subject alone. His eyes worried her. She felt they were piercing right through to her thoughts. Fanciful and silly. That's what came from a guilty conscience. Rick could not possibly have an inkling that she was planning to leave him; she couldn't be as transparent as that. Celia brightened her smile.

Susan returned with a fresh pot of tea. 'I hear some stockmen's wives are turning up later from the Harrison place . . . that right?'

'Yes, I meant to tell you earlier. Just a couple of women and some kids—their quarters went under water. It'll only be for a few days . . . Will you manage?' Rick asked, and Susan nodded. 'Good. The plane will be arriving around ten this morning.'

'We've already prepared everything, so they'll be no trouble, poor souls.'

A sudden shiver had shot down Celia's spine at the mention of the word 'plane'. Her heart raced slightly. 'Whose plane?' she asked, so casually she defied anyone to guess she had any particular interest in knowing.

Rick tossed her a curious look. 'Civilian Air Rescue . . . Why?'

Celia gave a squeaky laugh. 'No reason—I just wondered,' she glossed over it, a shade too airily, and immediately changed the subject to safer ground. She asked about the Harrisons, forgetting she had already asked the same question, and not listening to Rick's reply because her mind was busy on other things.

Rick left in one of the four-wheel drives, half an hour later. He kissed her casually on the verandah steps—in front of Susan and the two men going with him. There was no chance to say anything but a quick goodbye and given the precarious state of her emotions, that was probably just as well. Watching them drive away, Celia could have sat down on the steps and howled. She caught Susan's eye, watching her too intently and rallied a superficial smile. 'I have some things to attend to,' Celia said shortly and fled into the house.

Packing was merely a matter of throwing her toiletries into the still-unpacked suitcase. The hard part was working out what to say in the note she was going to leave for Rick. She worked on it in her head as she went about distractedly tidying up the room—unconsciously removing all traces that she had ever been there. With the plane due in less than twenty minutes, Celia finally sat down at the dressing table with a note pad and had the wastepaper basket filling up with umpteen abortive attempts at explanation when she heard the sound of the plane's engine.

Turning to a fresh page, she scribbled hastily:

'Our marriage was a mistake, but don't worry, I
will make sure that you get to keep my half of
Mandarah.' She signed it 'Celia' and read
through it quickly. Brusque. Churlish. It could
not have sounded worse if she'd tried, but there
was no time for another attempt and she couldn't
think of anything better in a rush anyway.
Perhaps the right words would come later and
she would write again from Sydney or England,
when she was far enough away from Rick and
Mandarah; when her mind was clear and she
didn't hurt so much.

Leaving the note on the dressing table Celia
slipped out through the french window for a
word to the pilot. Like a mother duck, Susan was
already leading the two women and three
children across the lawns to the house. Celia gave
them a wildly hearty wave as she sped to the
plane.

To her relief, the young pilot asked no
embarrassing questions, nor showed any surprise
at being asked for a lift. After ferrying people
around the countryside for the last week or so,
someone asking for a lift to the nearest town was
nothing out of the ordinary for him. 'Sure Mrs
Harland, happy to oblige. I'm heading to Mt Isa
to pick up supplies and air-drop them down to
tourists stranded along roadways. You wouldn't
believe the number of idiots dotted around the
place when the warnings went out weeks ago not
to travel along certain roads. Crazy!' He tapped
his forehead mockingly, then glanced at his
watch. 'I'd like to head off straight away, if that's
okay with you.'

'I'm all ready,' Celia assured him hastily. 'I'll just get my case and . . . attend to something.'

She planned to hand the envelope to Susan at the last moment. The old lady would have a fit but that couldn't be helped. Rick would have a fit too—but she would be well out of the way when that happened.

Her desperation to get herself into that plane was bordering on panic. It was irrational but Celia was not about to stop to analyse the frantic feeling. She raced back to the house and as she flung herself breathlessly into the room through the french window, Rick turned from the dressing table.

CHAPTER TEN

A strangled sound came out of her throat and for a timeless moment her feet glued her to the floor just inside the window as she stared, transfixed. 'What are you doing here?' she said shakily, recovering a little from her shock. Then as the paper crackled in Rick's hand, Celia realised what he had in the clenched fist and flew across the room. 'Give me that!' She made an unco-ordinated sweeping snatch at his hand.

Rick was much too quick and too strong for her. He raised the note easily out of reach and kept her at bay with his other hand. She grappled like a terrier in mindless fury, then suddenly stopped flailing at him and fell back in frustration. Rick had presumably read the note already so there was no point in trying to get it away from him now. 'You weren't meant to see it,' she said, beaten, but still angry.

'Not until after you'd left, you mean?' Rick said with a mirthless smile. She was flushed and out of breath while Rick looked unruffled and maddeningly calm.

'I thought you'd gone,' Celia bit out snappishly.

'Effective, wasn't it?' Rick bared his teeth wolfishly. It was not a smile.

'You had no intention of going to Keldon Downs again,' she accused with a not very logical feeling that she had somehow been wronged.

'Correction,' Rick sneered smoothly. 'I had every intention of going until your performance at breakfast when I twigged something was going on in that devious little mind of yours and thought it worth sending the chaps on without me.'

'That's a lie! If you'd really intended going you'd have taken the plane.' She wondered why that had not occurred to her before. If she'd put two and two together sooner she would have been waiting on the strip with her suitcase, ready to jump in immediately. 'You only wanted to catch me out.' She felt outraged that Rick had foiled her so neatly.

'That part is true,' Rick admitted with a sly curve of the mouth. 'It wasn't hard to work out what you were up to when you almost fainted with relief at the mention of the plane at breakfast.'

'That's despicable—and unfair!' she blurted hotly before she could stop herself and didn't need the contempt in Rick's eyes to remind her how hollow her accusation was.

Rick lunged at her. 'And what would you call this?' he demanded, brandishing the note angrily in front of her nose.

'I ... I was going to write again ...' she stammered, backing away from him.

'Oh were you just? That would have been a pleasant change from your usual disappearing act. Why the hell can't you talk about things for once, instead of always closing up and running away?' Rick swung sharply at the rap on the door. 'Yes?' he yelled at it.

They both stared as the door opened. Susan stood in the doorway. She eyed both of them in turn with equal lack of expression. 'Sorry to interrupt, but Pete—the pilot—asked me to check whether you needed help with your suitcase.' She looked at Celia with utter blandness.

Celia looked desperately out of the window to where a wing of the plane was just visible, then at her suitcase. Even as the wild temptation to make a bolt for it across the lawns catapulted through her mind, Rick stepped to her side and closed an arm around her shoulder, pressing down warningly. Her heart dived down with the last faint hope. Celia opened her mouth without knowing what was going to come out and did not get the chance to find out.

'Please tell Pete that Mrs Harland has changed her mind and won't be needing the lift,' Rick said in a voice that could have produced chilblains.

'I see,' Susan answered tonelessly, glinting eyes almost jumping out of their sockets with undisguised thrill, although by some anatomical feat the wrinkled face remained stolidly blank.

'Then please convey the message,' Rick said in a still very controlled voice and Susan did not wait to be told again.

'You can't stop me leaving,' Celia hissed in an undertone as soon as the door closed behind the housekeeper. She did not put it past the inquisitive old bird to have her ear, if not eye, glued to the keyhole. 'I just have,' Rick said smoothly but with something at the back of his eyes that made her shiver a little.

'This time,' Celia muttered mutinously and

twisted out from the imprisoning arm—quite easily, because Rick made no attempt to restrain her. 'You won't be able to next . . .'

'Shut up and start explaining,' Rick snapped her off with a bark.

Celia looked down at the paper he still held in his fist. 'I've explained in my letter.'

'Explained? In this?' he hollered, waving it at her.

'I . . . I would have written again to explain more fully.'

'Well, I'm saving you that trouble. Why don't you explain more fully to me now?' Rick suggested with menacing politeness, while his eyes tore strips off her and the rigid tension in his body told her it was costing him a lot to keep a grip on himself and not do what his eyes made only too plain that he wanted to do—beat the daylights out of her.

Tread carefully, Celia warned herself and moved away from him with a jerky display of casualness, to prove, mainly to herself, that she was not scared stiff. At the window she turned and faced him. 'Our marriage was a mistake,' she glossed over that bit hurriedly, expecting Rick to pull her up on it. 'And I was going to see the solicitor in Sydney to fix things up . . . legally.' She stopped to pick her next words.

'Yes? Do go on.'

'Damn it, if you'd stop sneering and mocking for one moment I might be able to,' she threw at him in heated frustration, momentarily forgetting her nervousness. 'I was going to see Mr Burgess to sign over my half of the property to you—so you wouldn't lose anything by our marriage breaking up.'

'I wasn't aware it had broken up,' Rick countered with poisonous restraint.

'No,' Celia agreed brittly, 'there hasn't been anything to break up, has there?' She made herself look him steadily in the eye. 'I don't want any part of it any more, Rick—our so-called marriage or Mandarah. I can't go on ... I'm sorry,' she said hopelessly, knowing he could have no idea what she was sorry about.

Rick's eyes flickered with what almost seemed like understanding from where she stood. 'I see,' he said, for the first time without anger or a hint of a sneer. 'And when did you decide all this ... or may I guess?' he smiled faintly.

'That doesn't matter,' she answered wearily. 'The point is, you'll have what you've always wanted. It's up to you whether you just take it ... or ...' she shrugged.

Rick's brows shot upwards. 'Or what ...?' he asked with sharpness—and puzzlement.

Celia chose her words with care. 'Or whether you compensate the family.' She watched nervously as his face darkened in a sweep of colour, then went on. 'Under the circumstances— since the marriage hasn't worked out ... you might offer to buy my share—I don't mean give me the money,' she put in quickly. 'I mean pay it into Sam's estate ... or something,' she trailed off having got to the point from which she couldn't extricate herself without bringing in words like 'self-respect' and 'fairness', and while Rick seemed to have calmed down, Celia was not prepared to risk those sort of words on him.

Rick gave an unexpected angry laugh. 'Those vultures you call relatives have got all they're going to get from me.' He opened his palm and stared down at the ball of crumpled paper. Very deliberately, he crumpled it into an even smaller ball and with unerring aim sent it flying into the wastepaper-basket by the dressing table. 'You're not leaving,' he said, almost conversationally.

'What did you say?' Celia brought out the words slowly, with pauses in between.

Rick glanced at her sharply. 'I said you're not leaving.'

She shook her head. 'No, before that . . . about the family.' Her eyes were narrowing in half-comprehension. 'You said . . .'

'I don't remember—it wasn't important,' Rick said dismissively. 'What is important is that . . .' He took a step towards her just as she sprang at him.

'You've paid them already! You've paid them off!' She would have shouted only the shock dragged her voice down to a harsh whisper.

'Don't be so bloody melodramatic.' Rick reacted angrily, stepping back from her. 'I didn't pay anybody off. It was a perfectly legal business transaction.'

'You bought your share!' Wild-eyed, she stared at him, so many things flying through her mind that she could not grasp any one of them.

'Sort of . . . yes.' It was an evasive answer and as Rick looked away from her Celia grabbed him by the arm.

'How ... sort of? And what about my share? Did you buy that too?' The inexplicable anger shook her from head to toe. Even her teeth were chattering with it.

Rick's face was flushed. 'I would have told you eventually ... I was going to tell you tonight.'

'So you did buy my share. You bought me out!' She stared at him for another moment then flung her hand off his arm and turned away. She felt duped—cheated.

Gripping her by the arms, Rick swung her around. 'No I did not. Your half is still yours—it's in your name ... it's exactly the same as if you'd inherited it,' he tried to explain with a seething urgency.

'It's not the same at all,' she screeched like a fishwife.

Rick shook her in frustration, his grip hurting her, while the shaking sent her hair flying wildly about her face. 'You little fool! What I did was for us. I did pay for Mandarah, but we own it jointly—just like any husband and wife.'

'You had no right to do it,' she hurled back at him. 'You took something that was mine and now you're saying it's all right because you've made me a present of it.'

With a despairing shake of the head, Rick dropped his arms and studied her outraged face with a curious twist of the mouth. 'Aren't you forgetting something?' Celia glared questionably. 'You didn't have any share unless you married me, so I could hardly take it away from you.'

The truth of that penetrated through the confusion of anger and hurt.

'Look, Celia,' Rick started again, reasonably. 'I had to do it this way. I couldn't have lived with myself if I had got the property through Sam's misguided will—and neither could you. You would have hated me for it—you have hated me because you thought that's exactly what I had done,' he amended without rancour. 'I wanted to tell you the truth but I had to wait until you'd worked out your own mixed-up motives for marrying me. You had to realise that it wasn't for Mandarah that you married me, but for myself. And you have realised it. You showed me that this morning.'

A fragile dormant hope was coming to life, but she was still hurting. 'Everybody knew, didn't they? That's why they were all so pleased about that wedding in the end ... they were getting their share regardless of the will. And I was the only one who didn't have a clue.'

'I asked—ordered them not to tell you,' Rick said in a strained voice.

'But why? Why didn't you tell me ... why did you have to blackmail me into the marriage? That was unfair!'

Rick grimaced, shrugged. 'And would you have married me if I had told you? If you had known that Mandarah was safe from being mined up whether you married me or not?'

Celia looked at him for a long time without speaking. 'Probably not,' she admitted at last.

Rick caught back a harsh laugh. 'No "probably" about it. You would have gone off, still on your high-horse, convinced that you hated me. I had to blackmail you, as you put it—

and quickly. The will was heaven-sent, and I couldn't get you away to Sydney quickly enough before you changed your mind. I was depending on Eleanor not to let you out of her clutches once you were down there,' he told her with a rueful smile. 'I know you resented that. It was a pretty mean thing to do, but I had to do it.'

'If it wasn't for the property, why did you marry me?' She knew the answer, only wanted to hear him say it aloud.

Rick's mouth curved faintly. 'Sometimes when you behave as idiotically as you're doing now, I ask myself the same question. I guess I'm just doomed to loving an idiot. I love you, Celia,' he said, with no trace of the smile, and with a kind of agony in his eyes.

She let the words seep in, wondering why she felt so utterly detached. She did not doubt what Rick had just said; given the circumstances, he had no other reason to marry her, but there was something unbudgeably angry in her mind. 'How long have you loved me?' she asked, so impersonally she might have been reading a question from a government form, and watched Rick's face impassively.

Rick looked slightly taken aback by her coldness. A wariness sprang into his eyes. 'Since you were about fifteen.' He smiled suddenly, in the belief that he had said the right thing, and that's when she hit him—on the top of the arm first, and then managed to land a closed fist on his chest in the second or two it took Rick to react and snatch up her hand.

'Then why the hell didn't you marry me when

I asked you? Why did you have to humiliate me like that? And make me hate you all those years.' She had no idea she was crying until she tasted salt on her lips.

Rick gathered her savagely up in his arms. She struggled mindlessly as he pushed her to the bed and with his arms still locked around her, pulled her down with him on to it. He held her tightly in her final moments of half-hearted struggle until she stopped, exhausted. Then they both lay very still, entwined together. In the silence the screech of a passing crow sounded piercingly loud.

Celia pushed her face out of his chest. 'Why didn't you marry me then?' she asked, drained.

Freeing one of his hands, Rick brushed the red tangle of hair from her face. 'How could I? You were still such a child.' He kissed a tear away from her cheek. Celia twisted her face from him. 'But I loved you,' she protested in almost a wail.

Easing himself up a little but covering her with his body, Rick looked down at her tear-stained face. 'Perhaps you did, but it wasn't the sort of love I wanted from you.' She frowned at him questioningly. 'Can't you understand, Celia? I was always part of your life ... first a big brother, then a surrogate father ... and then, that Christmas, just when I thought you'd actually started seeing me in a new light, you turned around and wanted me to be no more than a convenient rescuer. You wanted me to marry you so you wouldn't have to leave Mandarah—you practically said so in as many words.'

Celia shook her head agitatedly. 'It wasn't like that at all. I wanted to stay because I didn't want to leave you . . . because I loved you.'

Rick said with a burst of frustration. 'But I couldn't be certain of that. I wanted you then, Celia, believe me. You'll never know how desperately I wanted to make love to you—another second and I would have hanged the consequences. And then I was so angry—with you for being so . . . young and vulnerable and mixed up, and with myself for nearly taking advantage of that. I was horrible to you. I didn't mean to be.' Rick buried his face in her neck.

But she was not ready to give in to the pleading, arousing mouth—not yet. Celia said steadily. 'You let me go away, hating you.'

Rick raised his head and looked at her almost in surprise. 'I had to! George was right—you had to go away from this place . . . spread your wings. I had no right to keep you here . . . and I wanted you to learn to see me as a man—and love me as a man, and not as some sort of security symbol. I was prepared to wait a few more years. I wanted to tell you that . . . explain, but you wouldn't give me the chance.' Rick gave a dry laugh. 'I was scared witless there for a while thinking I'd lost you for good.'

That's what she had been so angry about; that's why she had lashed at him in that despairing rage—for the terrible risk Rick had taken with their future together. 'I might have married someone else.' She stared horrified into his eyes. 'Didn't that occur to you?'

'Of course the possibility of it occurred to me, but I wouldn't have let it happen,' Rick assured her. 'When you refused to have anything to do with me, I kept tabs on you through Sam. He knew how I felt about you, and kept me informed. I was ready to fly anywhere at a moment's notice if there had been any indication in your letters that you were becoming seriously interested in some guy.'

'Fat lot of use that would have done! Look what happened when you found Kel in my flat.' Celia reminded him huffily, not the least assured.

'It was the shock.' Rick had the grace to look sheepish. He grinned wryly. 'You can't blame me for flipping out when some guy opened the door to your flat, said you were in Paris for the week, and when I asked him what he was doing in your flat, told me he lived with you. It was a shock all right. I was on the first plane out before I knew what I was doing. When I got back here, Sam took ill and I couldn't get back to you. Believe me, Celia,' he said with deadly seriousness, 'I've never lived through a more terrible time than the last couple of months. Then when you came home and acted as if you'd like nothing better than to stick a very large knife in my back, I could have shouted with relief.'

Celia surprised herself with a sudden laugh. Rick went on, 'A woman doesn't want to inflict grievous bodily harm on a man unless she's in love with him. Mad Irishman or no, you were still in love with me enough to be angry.'

The smile faded off her face. 'About Kel.'

Shaking his head, Rick placed a finger over her lips. 'Don't talk about that ... please. I was insane with jealousy.' He tested out a smile, uncertainly. 'We macho gorillas often are, you know.'

She couldn't let him sweep that away with a joke. 'Would it have mattered if Kel and I really had been lovers?'

'How can you ask that?' Rick demanded with a spurt of anger. 'Yes, it would have mattered—a lot, but it wouldn't have made any difference to my wanting you.' He smiled a curious smile. 'To be honest, I felt more threatened by your hang-up about this place than by any man. I knew you loved me but I just didn't know how I was ever going to get you to admit it to yourself—that it was me you wanted, not Mandarah. I thought the other night . . . when you responded to me . . . before you closed up . . .'

So that's what Rick had meant. Mandarah, not Kel. 'I have admitted it, Rick,' she said softly. 'I love you.'

'I know. I knew that when you held me in your arms this morning. That's why I was going to explain everything to you tonight . . . that I had bought the place for us, and that you didn't have to resent me thinking I had married you for any tract of land or head of cattle. And then . . .' Rick's fingers sought the buttons of her blouse. 'And then I was going to make love to you.'

Celia shivered a little in deliberately suppressed excitement. She said, seriously, 'I never hated Mandarah more than I did last night when I thought that it stood between us.' She looked with wonder into Rick's eyes. How could she have ever thought he did not love her? She must have been blind.

'You'd better learn to love it again because we're well and truly stuck with it.' Rick examined her face with care, selected the tip of her nose and kissed it lightly. His mouth hovered above her lips. Celia put a finger to them and traced their outline lovingly, aware that Rick was aching with longing, and teasingly putting off the kiss. 'It must have cost a fortune,' she smiled.

'It did,' Rick agreed indifferently. 'We're saddled with a mortgage around our necks for the rest of our lives.'

Celia laughed and suddenly wrapping both her arms around Rick's neck, pulled his mouth down at last. 'For the rest of our lives . . .?' she murmured into his lips. 'I can't think of anything nicer.'

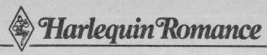 **Harlequin Romance**

Coming Next Month

2755   CINDERELLA WIFE   Katherine Arthur
The idea of pretending to be the adoring wife of a powerful
fashion mogul is bizarre. The possibility of having to give
him up in a year is heartwrenching.

2756   GIRL OF MYSTERY   Mons Daveson
An Australian millionaire is mystified by a secretive waif
who dashes in front of his Jaguar. She won't tell him her
address; so he feels compelled to take her home.

2757   AEGEAN ENCHANTMENT   Emily Francis
A physiotherapist loves Greece! But her patient's older—
and hopelessly overbearing—brother insists she will never
understand their ways and can't belong. Which only makes
her more determined than ever to fit in.

2758   HUNGER   Rowan Kirby
When a Canadian writer and his troubled daughter invade
an English bookshop owner's solitude, can she balance her
hunger for love with her fear of being hurt again?

2759   PAGAN GOLD   Margaret Rome
Valley D'Oro's mining magnate accuses a visiting
Englishwoman of squandering her family's fortune to trap a
man of substance. Yet he defends his family tradition of
purchasing brides from impoverished aristocrats!

2760   SKY HIGH   Nicola West
An amateur hot-air balloonist refuses to be grounded by an
unfair job interview. She knows exactly where she wants to
be: suspended somewhere between heaven and earth—in
this man's arms.

Available in April wherever paperback books are sold, or
through Harlequin Reader Service.

In the U.S.
P.O. Box 1397
Buffalo, N.Y.
14240-1397

In Canada
P.O. Box 2800, Postal Station A
5170 Yonge Street
Willowdale, Ontario M2N 6J3

WORLDWIDE LIBRARY IS YOUR TICKET TO ROMANCE, ADVENTURE AND EXCITEMENT

Experience it all in these big, bold Bestsellers— Yours exclusively from WORLDWIDE LIBRARY WHILE QUANTITIES LAST

To receive these Bestsellers, complete the order form, detach and send together with your check or money order (include 75¢ postage and handling), payable to WORLDWIDE LIBRARY, to:

In the U.S.
WORLDWIDE LIBRARY
901 Fuhrmann Blvd.
Buffalo, N.Y. 14269

In Canada
WORLDWIDE LIBRARY
P.O. Box 2800, 5170 Yonge Street
Postal Station A, Willowdale, Ontario
M2N 6J3

Quant.	Title	Price
_____	**WILD CONCERTO**, Anne Mather	$2.95
_____	**A VIOLATION**, Charlotte Lamb	$3.50
_____	**SECRETS**, Sheila Holland	$3.50
_____	**SWEET MEMORIES**, LaVyrle Spencer	$3.50
_____	**FLORA**, Anne Weale	$3.50
_____	**SUMMER'S AWAKENING**, Anne Weale	$3.50
_____	**FINGER PRINTS**, Barbara Delinsky	$3.50
_____	**DREAMWEAVER**, Felicia Gallant/Rebecca Flanders	$3.50
_____	**EYE OF THE STORM**, Maura Seger	$3.50
_____	**HIDDEN IN THE FLAME**, Anne Mather	$3.50
_____	**ECHO OF THUNDER**, Maura Seger	$3.95
_____	**DREAM OF DARKNESS**, Jocelyn Haley	$3.95

	YOUR ORDER TOTAL	$_____
	New York and Arizona residents add appropriate sales tax	$_____
	Postage and Handling	$ .75
	I enclose	$_____

NAME _____

ADDRESS _____ APT.# _____

CITY _____

STATE/PROV. _____ ZIP/POSTAL CODE _____
WW-1-3